Blood Life

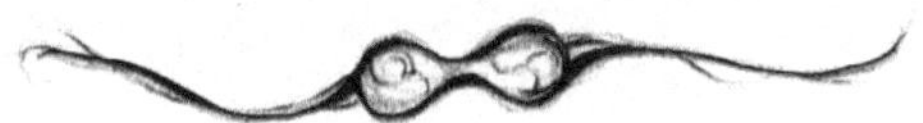

Turnabout Volume II

RUSS WOOD

So now I was loocked in my room. Then I had an idea to make some robots. So I did. Then I had another idea to climb out the window the biggest robot turned into a spase ship. Then we landed at a restsrant we paid for it. Then we got to work eating.

When we were done we went out in the woods. Then we had a place to sleep but we had bad dreams. My dream was about! My robots were in a spell. And chased me!!!!

But when I woke up I woke upon the wrong side of the bed. Then I noutist that my hair grew a little. Then I told my robots that I was going for a walk.

Then I met two men and they were plice men. They throwd me in the car and took me home.

So that was a story.

THE END

I assure everyone my parents were the most patient, loving parents a child could ask for. This was just an example of a young kid coming up with the most dramatic story he could fathom in his protected little world.

Anyway, thanks to Mom, Dad, and my siblings for not forcing me to see the ocean for the first time in my life and encouraging me in this path I started.

I don't think I would have been a good surfer.

Acknowledgements

When I was about six or seven, my family borrowed a motorhome and went on a trip to Disneyland. I have vague memories of Disneyland, but one thing I remember clearly was a set of scented markers that we brought along. The tip of my nose was multi-colored midway through the first day.

I had found some paper and masking tape in the cabinets and decided I would make a book. Apparently, I was so into writing my first book that I opted to stay in the motorhome and write rather than go to the beach.

I think I might even still have it around here somewhere. Hold on…

Found it, among my *Indiana Ninja* and *Army Tales* books! Okay, here's the words from my very first book:

Once upon a time when I was three years old I found a bottle full of somting. I drinked it then I became famos! I was so happy that I screemed out I'm famos Mom and Dad said hold the nois down. They were jellis too so my dad kicked me down hit me and jumped right on me. My mom shuved me in the door and slamed it on me.

DEDICATION

To Mike Wood, the guy who eats weeds.
www.wildutahedibles.com

now, having been given a drink of water and some fruit. Marai didn't want to wake her. She knew how her mom would take this. Instead, Marai bent down and kissed her gently on the cheek.

"I love you, mom," she said quietly.

Joshua was now pacing over by the trees. Marai went to him and laid a gentle hand on his shoulder. He stopped and looked her straight in the eyes.

"Thank you," Marai said.

Joshua just nodded. Marai turned and walked away from him.

"You're my best friend," he said to her back. Marai nodded and took a few steps out onto the water's surface until she was over a deep spot.

"Where are you going?" Kent asked, stirring from his nap.

"I'm going to renew Hope," Marai said.

She let herself sink, filled her lungs with water, and died.

THE END

IMPORTANT AUTHOR'S NOTE

This book is comprised of two separate but connected stories. You may start with either story and then flip the book over and read the other. Depending on which side you start on, the title is either *Blood Life*, or *Lifeblood*. Your experience with the stories might differ from someone who has read it in the opposite order.

So make your choice…

WOOD/LIFEBLOOD

Marai looked up at the slivered moon, barely visible in the blue sky.

She knew her mother would be safe. Joshua was a good friend, who had *already* tried to sacrifice his life to save her mother's. He was tending to her even now, as they rested on the far shore.

Marai also knew that the greater war was just beginning. Sayid had vowed the people of Earth would "wipe the planet clean and start over," and Marai sorrowed at what that meant for the people of Hope.

She also knew there were still other Lamek tribes in the rainforest, who worshipped the Destroyer just as this one did. Surely, the high priest would gather them together again to further the work of death and destruction.

Mostly, Marai had to know if what she believed was really true. Was her faith strong enough that she would be willing to give everything to test it?

How far *could* she go? She was determined to find out, even if it meant what she thought it did.

Marai got up from the grassy bank and walked over to where her mother lay. She was sleeping peacefully

1

Hugh Winters was never late for work. Thirty-four years of working under the President and he had never *once* come through the doors any later than 15 minutes early. As Chief Judge, it was expected of him to be punctual. Many of the President's more important tasks fell to him, so he made sure to set more than one alarm in his room, including the one on his phone.

Which made this morning all the more frustrating. A power outage must have knocked out his nightstand clock—and kept it off, judging by the current lack of a display—but, as bad luck would have it, his phone battery had to die on the very same night, probably due to a lack of charge. Fortunately, Hugh's internal clock prompted him to awaken only twenty-five minutes later than usual, so there was still a chance he could be to work on time if he skipped his shower. He picked up his landline to call the power company as he rushed about getting dressed, but even the landline was down, which didn't strike Hugh strange at the time. He just heard no audible tone coming

WOOD/LIFEBLOOD

A giant, dark shadow passed underneath them.

"What was that?!" Kent asked.

"Hold still!" Marai repeated.

The warrior nearest them raised a stone knife into the air in anticipation of the kill and then suddenly shot underneath the surface. A large, red bubble emerged where he had stood.

The warriors directly behind him halted, confused. One warrior's eyes widened.

Suddenly, a giant fish with sharp teeth rose up underneath them, swallowing them whole. The other Lamek started to retreat, but their movement attracted more giant fish, which started to thrash the water in a feeding frenzy. One by one, the Lamek warriors were swallowed up.

Almost as soon as it started, it stopped. All that remained as evidence that the warriors existed were ripples on the water.

Marai could see the solitary figure of the high priest standing on the far shore, now helpless to stop them.

"Uh… can we get the holy crap off of this lake now?" Kent asked.

from the phone receiver, and hung up so as not to waste any more time thinking about it. Hugh would just have to go about the day with no clues as to when the power would be restored.

He lived alone on ten acres of fenced pasture about thirty miles outside of the city of Capital, and he would have to speed on the highway in order to make up for lost time. He jumped into his car and pushed the ignition button. Nothing. He tried again. Still nothing. He tried to manually start the car with the key, but the starter refused to turn over.

"Oh, come on!" Hugh cried aloud to nobody. "Is *everything* broken today?"

Hugh got out of the car and slammed the door shut. He stood with his hands on his hips, thinking about his next move. He couldn't use the phone, and there was no way to charge his car battery without power.

At the end of his long driveway was the old highway, and Hugh decided he would run down there and hitch a ride into the city with the next car to pass by. The road was normally pretty busy at this time of day, with people making their way to the capitol for work, and chances were good he might even know some of the drivers. He jogged down the tree-lined lane, cursing the sweat that was now wetting his shirt underneath his suit.

walking across the surface. Kent laughed like a child at play until he looked back and saw the Lamek gathering along the shore, led by the high priest.

"I hope they're not good swimmers," he said.

The Lamek all took sharp stones and sliced them across the soles of their feet, creating clouds of crimson blood underneath them when they stepped out onto the water's surface.

"Uh, Marai…" Kent said.

She looked back and saw them gaining on her little group. Every one of them except the high priest was now on the water, running after them. She remembered something from her time before.

It was time for her to call in a favor from Creation. She turned them around to face the Lamek pursuers.

"Have you ever seen a lake monster?" she asked Joshua and Kent.

"Hey, how about let's keep moving?" Kent said.

The Lamek were within twenty yards of them and closing the gap very quickly. Kent tried to pull her hand toward the opposite shore.

"Hold still," Marai said.

He should have *at least* taken the time to apply deodorant!

When he reached the end of his driveway, he was not met with the sounds of traffic, but instead with a sight that led him to believe his problems were not limited to himself alone. Along both sides of the highway a number of cars were parked, some still in the roadway. None of the cars had passengers, and when Hugh jogged down and felt the cold hood of the nearest car, he believed the cars had stopped working in the middle of the night. Why none of the drivers had stopped in to ask him for help, he couldn't guess, but at least now he *knew* something strange had happened in the area, and he realized the President probably needed him now more than ever.

What could possibly have caused cars to stop working also? Hugh thought, as he ran back to his barn. *This goes beyond just a power outage.*

Hugh saddled up Babe and mounted her. Twenty miles galloping would be tough on the old nag, but Dusty was still too green to take into a city. Hugh kicked her sides and they took off down the road.

An hour and a half later, Hugh rode up in front of the side security gate. Besides the crowd he saw her. He said it was her belief that held her up, not her lightness, so what difference should a body make? But *did* she believe?

"What are we waiting for?" Kent asked, as the nearest warriors broke through the trees a few dozen yards away.

Marai knew it was decision time.

Xrys had told her before that if she lacked the faith she needed, sometimes, just *wishing* to believe would do. *What if...*

Marai closed her eyes and imagined the water line being much farther away. *It's just more land,* she told herself. She took a step and didn't sink. She suppressed her surprise, afraid that it might be another form of doubt. She took another step, still atop the surface of the water.

"Marai, what are you doing?" Joshua asked.

"Quick, I need you to hold my hand and step out onto the water, believing it will hold you."

"I don't know if I can believe that," Joshua said.

She reached out and grabbed his hand anyway. Kent took her other hand. "Then I will believe for all of us," she said.

They stepped out onto the water and started

emptying a supermarket on his way, the ride through the city had been eerily silent. He realized that the usual din of horns, construction, and sirens were missing.

"I was wondering if you'd show up, your honor," the security guard said.

"It's my job to show up," Hugh said. "*Especially* on days like today."

"Very good, sir."

"Is the Cabinet here?" Hugh asked.

"As many as live nearby, your honor. There's still a few unaccounted for."

"Hmm. Well, I'd better get in there. Will you see to it that my…vehicle gets parked somewhere safe?"

"Very good, sir," the guard said. He nervously took the reigns while Hugh dismounted and walked through the gate to the palace.

Hugh stood inside the doorway of the situation room, while a few members of the Cabinet were gathered in a meeting with President Paul Wyndham. A lower judge entered into the room carrying a handwritten note to the President, which he read while the lower judge exited the room, saluting Hugh on the way out.

heart, trusting that everything would turn out right, because that's how it was *destined* to be. But now, she found it hard to find anything but despair in their situation. She hung her head.

"Someone is beckoning to us across the lake," Joshua said.

Marai lifted her head and saw a distant figure walking along the far shore. He had pure white hair and was dressed in a loincloth. He beckoned to them again. The sounds of the pursuing Lamek grew louder.

Marai remembered the time she had spirit walked across the lake with Xrys. Whether it was a dream or hallucination, it had felt so real…just as real as now. She was still unsure if *Xrys* had been real, but now she had to make a decision, and it might just be a decision of which way to die; by the hands of the Lamek, or by drowning.

If Xrys was real and *if* she could spirit walk, she was not a spirit now, and therefore made of much denser matter. Not only that, but she had others with her, some of whom she knew didn't believe in supernatural abilities. But Xrys had taught her to believe the water would support her, even though nothing in her past experience should cause her to believe it would, and the water held

"Some are reporting the outage is worldwide," President Wyndham said. "Thus, eliminating the possibility of another nation attacking us."

"How would we know if that were the case?" Mel, the Secretary of Technology said. Hugh didn't care much for Mel, who seemed to always want to show off how much he knew by telling everyone so. But he did have a good point. "The fastest any message could travel since the outage would be...well..."

"By horseback," Hugh said, announcing his presence.

"Ah, Hugh, you made it," President Wyndham said, looking up from the handwritten report. "Excuse me gentlemen, I must have a word with the Chief Judge in my chambers."

They walked into the President's private chambers and the President locked the door behind them.

"Come in, Hugh. Have a seat," he said, beckoning him to sit in a couch in the center of the room. President Wyndham sat in the chair adjacent him, rather than behind the desk. He wore a concerned look on his face.

"How long have we known each other, Hugh?" he asked.

"Let's see...we met a little before your coronation, so...about thirty some years now," Hugh

XVIII

"I can't go any further," Kent wheezed as they reached the lake. The sun was starting to rise over the mountain.

"You all keep going, I'll stay back here and fight off the savages." He wearily picked up a handful of pebbles and a twig, wielding it like a knife and turning around on the trail.

"We're not leaving you here, Kent!" Marai said, slapping the twig out of his hands.

Marai knew she didn't have the energy to help them all spirit walk. They *had* to rest, but the enemy would be upon them and kill them if they did. Joshua must have been exhausted, carrying Kit. Marai had to get her mother to safety. She was fading from malnutrition.

Marai could hear the Lamek, making their way up the mountain, and wished the things she had once believed were true. How much better it was to carry hope in her said. He knew it had been exactly thirty-four years, but he didn't want it to seem like he had kept track.

"Yes, we were a lot younger then," President Wyndham said. "You still look like the same young man, albeit with gray streaks in your hair now."

I have gray in my hair? Hugh thought. He hadn't been paying much attention to himself in the mirror lately.

"You've always been so reliable. I feel like I can trust you with anything I assign you to do," the President continued. "But I'm going to ask you to do something for me as a friend, off the books."

"It wouldn't be the first time," Hugh replied.

"Yes, I know…and that's why I feel like I can ask you now."

"What would you have me do?"

"Mel was right in there: We don't know if this outage is worldwide or if it was an act of war by one of the pro-secession nations. Regardless, I'm going to employ all means available to assemble our military and preemptively quash any would-be rebels in other nations, even if it means hand-to-hand combat."

"And how does this concern me?" Hugh asked.

"Oh, that part of my plan doesn't. I just wanted you to know. I am leaving the palace in charge of my

Marai appeared in front of them and said, "Fast? I've been waiting here for hours!" They started to run together. Kit made groaning noises, which assured them all she was alive, but unwell. Marai fell back and kissed her mother on the head.

"Marai, what happened in there?" Joshua asked as soon as they felt they could slow their pace.

"I took your signal and went into my light walk, disarming all the village. Then I fended off an attack by a hideous priest before I came and touched you."

"I wanted you to *escape*," Joshua said. "I was trying to create a diversion while you grabbed your mom and got away!"

"I couldn't reach her, Joshua!"

"Did you kill Sayid, too?" he asked.

"I don't know what happened," Marai said. "He just… died!"

Kent was gasping for air next to them, "I'll have to tell you about that…when I'm not running for my life."

They heard the sounds of pursuit a few hundred yards behind, and they started running in earnest.

"Where are we going?" Joshua asked.

"To the Sacred Mountain!" Marai yelled.

brother, the Prime Minister, while I go hide in an 'undisclosed location.'"

"The Wheel House?"

"Undisclosed to any but my best friend, of course," the President said, chuckling. Then he turned serious. "Hugh, a few days ago an unidentified craft landed in the southern part of Pangaea, somewhere near Montsacre in Congo."

"What do you mean, unidentified?"

"I mean; this came from space."

"*After* we shot down the meteor with the interception missile?"

"That's just it…I'm not sure that even *was* a meteor, now that this other craft appeared."

"Why didn't we just shoot *it* down?" Hugh asked.

"It's not as simple as that," President Wyndham said. "We saw the 'meteor' coming a month out and had time to prepare for it. Shooting it down was a complicated matter of planning to intercept the trajectory and having the missile in-place beforehand. The problem is…when the 'meteor' passed behind the moon, satellite imagery shows a huge decrease in size when it emerged from the other side, but we had already launched the missile before we had a chance to investigate the discrepancy any further.

"I decided to pass along to the media only that the

torch fire, and the flames quickly ascended the rope, catching the bridge on fire. This caused the Lamek running down the walkway from the upper caves to turn around and retreat.

Lamek started pouring from the ground-level caves in pursuit of Joshua. He tucked the knife away and ran toward the gate, not knowing how he would open it when he got there, since he was still carrying Kit. Behind him to the right, he heard someone gaining on them. Joshua braced himself and prepared to fight. He timed his turn so that he could catch his pursuer off-guard, but it was *he* who was unprepared. The man sprinted right past him, and yelled at Joshua as he passed.

"Don't stop, you idiot!" It was Kent!

Joshua could see many warriors in close pursuit, and he turned back around to run. Kent had reached the gate and had managed to crack it open slightly. Joshua started running for the opening with all he was worth. He managed to slip through with Kit, and Kent grunted as he pushed it shut, just as the mob arrived. Joshua leaned back against the gate as Kent pushed over a heavy pole with a rotted base, bracing it against the side.

"Pretty fast, huh?" Kent asked.

threat of a meteorite had been destroyed because—as you well know—I needed a victory to rally Hope around my leadership. Given the current wars and uprisings, there was a common enemy, threatening us all and giving us a chance to unite once again. But…"

"But it wasn't just a meteor." Hugh said.

"I don't think it is," President Wyndham said. He looked Hugh directly in the eyes and said, very soberly, "I think we're being scouted for an alien invasion."

"Which brings us to me," Hugh said.

"Yes, which brings us to you."

"What do you want me to do when I find them?"

"Judge them," President Wyndham said. "Find out what they are doing here, and if you perceive them to be a threat, eliminate them."

"Near Montsacre, in Congo, right?"

"Right. Do you want to me to send along a squad of lower judges with you?"

"Not needed; I have my own backup. A whole legion if need be."

"Or you could just go it alone," President Wyndham said. "After all, you can kill without using your hands."

"Only the wicked," Hugh said.

suddenly his mind was filled with survival scenarios. On the Exodus, he had been preparing for a planet larger than Earth, and Hope was slightly *smaller*. Gravity didn't have as much pull on him. He looked up at the cage Marai's mom was in and leaped up, grabbing onto the cage with both hands. He swung his legs until the cage was swinging over the bridge, and sliced through the ropes on the bottom, opening the cage and sending them both tumbling onto the wooden walkway.

The soul eater nearest them charged, pulling a knife from his loin cloth. Joshua was afraid he had lost his martial arts skills, and would be helpless to defend himself. The soul eater slashed his knife at Kit, who still lay on the walkway.

A loud "crack" sounded in the air, and the soul eater flew off the walkway backward. Joshua didn't have time to wonder what had happened, he just picked up Kit in a fireman's carry and started running to the end of the bridge. Some soul eaters appeared, climbing up the rope ladder at the end. Joshua quickly used the knife to cut the rope railing, which he used to swing down to the village floor, still holding Kit. He felt so much stronger with the lighter pull of gravity! He put the end of the dry rope into

2

Hugh decided he would release Tai and Borghaus from captivity and take them along with him to Congo.

Tai was originally from Congo, and had come to the north on a killing spree that included a member of the Cabinet. Whether he had intentionally targeted the Cabinet member or had just been killing another random victim made no difference to Hugh when he passed judgment on Tai. Regardless of his past, Tai would be a valuable resource in Hugh's current assignment. Tai knew the area of Congo as well as the languages and had spent years tracking animals for guided hunts before he moved on to tracking more dangerous game for his own twisted pleasure.

Borghaus, on the other hand, was a large, silent man who had spent many years in the military serving as head of security for the classified governmental research facility in Sa'ara. He had access to all of the research and had been selling government secrets for large sums of money to enemies of the state. When he

The blade of the knife had stopped an inch short of piercing Kent's neck. Marai fell back and caught her breath.

The world was eerily silent now, after having been through a battle on the other side of the veil of life. It almost didn't seem real; more like a fitful nightmare. It seemed like it had lasted for hours, but she had probably only been out for a few seconds. She couldn't dwell on it now, or she would risk coming out of her trance. She would have to take time to figure it all out later.

Marai stood and twisted the knife from the priest's grip, hoping she would break some of his fingers in real-time. She ran over to Joshua and stood in front of him, still breathing hard, then reached out and held his hand.

Joshua saw Marai appear in front of him with tattered clothes and scratches on her face and neck. She didn't speak any words, just placed a knife in his free hand and nodded upward to her mother. He understood.

When she let go, everyone in the village sprang to life, but Marai remained hidden. Joshua was surprised to see Sayid was dead and the villagers were unarmed, and was finally discovered, he sliced his way through dozens of people as he made his escape, and nobody could bring him down.

Nobody except for Hugh, that is.

Hugh intercepted him as he was trying to board a plane in New York. Security had missed the bone blades Borghaus was able to keep on his person throughout his career, and just as he passed through the security gate, Hugh stood before him and called his name. Borghaus was found guilty the instant he pulled the blades from his coat.

Hugh had imprisoned him, but now he needed his services. Borghaus never let on how intelligent he actually was, and how he understood every secret he sold, so he could evaluate their worth. Included in those secrets were extra-terrestrial studies that might be of value to Hugh, now that his mission involved possible alien encounters.

Hugh thought about how odd it was that he might be dealing with an alien species. Throughout the whole history of Hope, nobody had ever accomplished interstellar space travel, and now they might be facing a threat from beings with technology way beyond their own. Not only that, but all the people of Hope were now theoretically without any sort of technological advantage death, made her confused and weak. She couldn't even struggle against her captors anymore. *It will not be long now…*

A familiar, husky voice rang out, "Hang on, Marai!" She looked toward the altar and saw Kent run up and grab the priest off of her. Suddenly, she could feel strength enter her spirit as her body drew breaths again. She could feel her body willing her spirit to rejoin it. With the strength of this connection to a physical body, she easily shook off the disembodied, weaker spirits and ran full speed to her body, diving in.

She opened her eyes. To Marai's side, Kent struggled to keep a chokehold on the disfigured priest. The priest slapped the spiked in his arms, garnering enough strength to pull himself free from Kent's grasp. She gathered her thoughts into one purpose and tossed them out.

Marai had acted just in the nick-of-time. The priest had gone into the alternate time-flow and was picking up the knife off the ground. Kent was frozen in time, helpless. Marai ran up behind the priest, jumped on his back, and grabbed the spike with both hands. The priest froze instantly in place as Marai pulled the spike free.

in a potential war. He had seen a lot in his many years, but nothing that rivaled this. Could this be a sign that "The End" was near?

The three of them slowly made their way through Capital, each criminal tethered to Hugh as they walked beside his horse. The uneasy silence was only broken by a noisy flock of birds flying over their heads.

"Hey, boss…" Tai said in his broken English accent.

"What?" answered Hugh, roughly. He didn't have much patience for Tai, but he needed him.

"Why the birds fly the wrong way?"

Hugh looked up and noticed the migratory birds were, indeed, flying the wrong direction for the time of year. "Confused, I guess. I don't know. Keep moving."

Tai shrugged his shoulders and trudged on.

After a while, Hugh noticed Tai staring at him. Tai's eyes met his and must have took it as an invitation to talk. "That a shiny gold badge you got on you chest, boss," Tai said.

"It's my Chief Judge badge. There aren't many like it. Now lock it up."

They passed by the same store Hugh had seen earlier, tucked into the corner of a shopping center. Hugh observed how the run on the store had now escalated to spirit apart. Marai was being dragged away from her body, and she felt her connection weakening. The priest was about to choke out the final connection she had with her body, as she kept being pulled farther and farther away.

"I can see the girl!" a spirit shouted from underneath a pile of Lamek. "Help her!"

Marai heard someone let out a mighty roar, and fell to the ground when her captors were violently swept away. A giant man swung at the spirits all around to keep them at bay. He looked down at her and shouted, "Go!"

Marai jumped up and attempted to run over to where the priest still straddled her body, and once more, evil spirits caught hold of her and began pulling her away. There were too many! Everything was happening in a flurry of action. Her efforts to fight free were useless!

She glanced over and noticed the large spirit who had tried to help her was now being restrained.

Suddenly, a legion of spirits fell from the sky and began combatting the dark spirits. A great war took place before her eyes, but those who held her began to pull her away from the fray, rather than release her to join the battle.

The growing distance, and her body's imminent

looting. Some common thugs were carrying electronics out of broken store windows, and others were fighting over worthless items. It seemed odd to him how quickly things had escalated out of hand. Normally, a power outage would have to last for weeks before there was such unrest.

"Are you not going to judge them, boss?" Tai asked Hugh.

"I'll leave this to the lower judges," Hugh said. "It's not like the things they're stealing are going to do them much good without power, anyway."

"But maybe this blackout be over tomorrow," Tai said.

"Then why are they looting?" Hugh said. "Is there some other event that's making them take advantage of a blackout?"

"Hey, if you untether me, I go bring down a few," Tai said. "You could make me like you deputy."

"You're lucky I released you at all," Hugh said.

"Yes, *lucky* me," Tai said.

Hugh suddenly stopped and lifted a hand to silence Tai.

"What you seeing, boss," Tai asked. "Maybe you untether me and I go…"

"Shut up, you fool," Borghaus said. The intervention of the usually quiet man seemed to be enough were able to perceive time differently, but there was still one thing she had experienced that he *hadn't* explained: Spirit walking.

She closed her physical eyes, and opened her spiritual eyes, hoping it would not be permanent.

Whether it was a hallucination, fabrication, or real didn't matter to her now. She would try *anything* to save her mother's and Joshua's lives.

All around her, she believed she could see the spirits of departed Lamek, and they seemed to be engaging a couple of other spirits in a scuffle. Next to her, she could see the spirit of Sayid kneeling next to his body, looking at his hands with a shocked expression on his face. This could all be real, or it could be the random firings of a brain deprived of oxygen. Regardless, she determined to act. She could pass through the grasp of the priest now, so she stood and grabbed at the spike. Her hands passed through his head with no effect! Her spirit matter was not dense enough to manipulate objects in the real world. Before she could attempt to remove the spike from his head again, she was set upon by spirits who were now aware of her presence. They shouted their battle cries, drunken with bloodlust, and it felt like they would tear her to silence Tai.

"That woman…" Hugh said, looking at the parking lot. A woman with two small children hiding behind her was trying to pull her loaded shopping cart away from two young men.

"Stay put," Hugh told Tai and Borghaus. He dismounted and crossed the parking lot in a few hurried strides.

"Hey!" he shouted. The youths let go of the cart and wheeled on him, ready for action. The shorter of the two started advancing toward Hugh. The woman took advantage of their inattention to rush her cart and children down the street. The young man looked back at her and then turned to Hugh in a rage.

"Oh, you just signed your death warrant, old man!" he said. He swung a wild haymaker at Hugh's face, and he leaned back slightly to easily dodge it. The momentum caused the youth to reel clumsily and almost lose his balance. He righted himself and prepared to throw another swing.

This time, the taller youth grabbed his friend in a hug from behind, pinning his arms to his sides.

"Hey, what are you doing, man?!"

"Don't, Rayce!" the taller one warned. "That's Chief Judge Winters!"

flow, despite her inability to clear her mind. How could he do what she did, but with more power?

All of the things she had learned about the soul eaters came to her mind at once. She remembered how they sacrificed part of their physical bodies in order to gain spiritual abilities. This man had no facial features and was burned all over his body. The spikes in his arms must have given him the inhuman strength with which he held her down. He was a true believer in the Destroyer, and somehow, he had been given the same ability as Marai and Joshua.

But what exactly are we doing?

"We're both interrupting the processes of timekeeping in the left hemispheres of our brains in order to perceive the passage of time at different rates."

Joshua's words came clearly to her mind. She looked up at the priest's head and noticed a metal spike protruding from the left side of his head. She tried to reach for it but he pushed her hand to the ground.

"I need no knife to kill you," he said. He began squeezing her throat again. She could feel the life slipping from her.

Joshua had been able to explain to her how they

Rayce's eyes grew wide and the fight seemed to flee his body. "The Black Judge?" he asked.

"Yes, you don't want to mess with *him!*"

Rayce angrily tried to free himself from his friend's grasp. "Don't you think I know that?!" he shouted. "Let go of me!"

After freeing himself, he pulled his sleeves back down over his arms and looked at the ground, as if he hoped his last outburst didn't excite Hugh.

Rayce cleared his throat and said, "We're sorry, Your Honor."

"Go home, boys," Hugh warned. Without argument, they turned and left.

They arrived at Hugh's house in the middle of the night, and Hugh was surprised to see a light shining from a basement window.

"You have power?" Tai asked.

"No…I don't," Hugh replied, as he pulled up on Babe's reigns. He dismounted and absently patted her on the neck, never taking his eyes off his house. Sounds of items being rummaged through came from the open front door.

Joshua, still frozen in place. Sayid bent his arm as if he was preparing to draw his weapon. Joshua was about to die.

She could do nothing to escape the clutches of the burned priest. In all of her efforts to disarm their antagonists, she had missed the one who would surely put an end to Joshua's life. It couldn't end like this!

Help him! Marai cried out in her mind. The words brought the world back to normal speed. Now, she was truly helpless.

And then, without warning, Sayid crumpled to the ground, staring up at the sky with lifeless eyes. He was dead.

The grip around her throat tightened, and Marai turned her attention back to the gruesome priest, who now held the knife in a raised position. She managed to fight a foot free and touch the earth with her big toe. A tiny amount of light entered in and froze the world again, including the priest this time. She managed to remove his hand from her throat and sit up. She knocked the knife from his hand and it fell near Sayid's body. Marai stepped back onto the ground and started walking to Joshua, when the priest suddenly became animated and pulled her roughly to the ground. He held her in the alternate time-

"You wanted to help?" Hugh asked Tai.

"Oh, *now* you need me?" Tai said.

"Yes, now I have need of you," Hugh said condescendingly. "Go in there and take a look at who's rummaging around through my storage."

"Can I hurt him?"

"Just *look*, and then report back to me." Hugh untethered Tai and set him off toward the house. "Don't try to run," he added.

"What you do if I did?" Tai called back.

"Do you ever want to eat again?" Hugh asked.

Tai didn't answer, just turned around and walked brazenly toward the front door. He stepped inside without even pausing, as if it was his own house. It irked Hugh how arrogant Tai could act.

The sounds of the rummaging stopped and Hugh started to be concerned Tai had done something foolish. He started leading Babe closer to the house. Someone was coming back up the stairs, visible from the open door. It was Tai.

"What did you do?" Hugh asked.

"Nothing, boss!" Tai said. "I think he get what he came for and he wrapping things up."

"Who?"

"I do not know. Some guy with a lantern who

two cold hands grabbed her from behind. She was turned around violently to face her assailant. A horribly burned man with no eyes, nose, or mouth held her firmly in his grip. He had spikes protruding from various parts of his body, and wore a priestly shock of scarlet cloth over his shoulder. Marai screamed.

His head tilted back to open his mouth, and a deep voice sounded from within.

"The Destroyer requires your blood."

Marai couldn't understand why he was able to move through time at her speed. The world remained still around them, but she was now assaulted with noises coming from the man's open mouth, like many screaming voices. He began to push her backward, and Marai found it was useless to fight against his push. She felt something solid behind her, and realized he was putting her upon his altar. Despite her furious struggle, he managed to separate her feet from the ground and lay her down.

She went to pull the knife from her belt, but was shocked to see the man already held it in his hand. He pressed his other hand deep into her throat, and she started to gasp for air. The world started slowly returning to its normal speed around her, and she looked over at wants your guns really bad."

The stairwell became lighter and footsteps could be heard ascending the steps. Tai dramatically bowed to Hugh, as if to say, "I told you so." The thief ran out the front door with an armload of rifles and a full backpack on his back. He froze when he saw Hugh standing in front of him.

"Is there a reason you think you need my stuff more than I do?" Hugh said. He recognized the man in the torchlight as a neighbor. A somewhat portly man named Louis.

"I…," the man said.

"You what?"

"I didn't *want* to steal from you, Hugh," he said.

"Then why on Hope *are* you?"

"Everyone has been talking about the meteor, saying it's a sign of the end, and since the outage, well…everyone's getting scared. Doing things to each other. I've heard they're looting and rioting in the city, and I had no way of protecting my family."

"So being scared of thieves justifies you becoming one?" Louis was visibly shaking.

"I…I thought maybe you were dead. I saw you leave this morning and when you didn't come back…"

"Judge him already," Tai said.

WOOD/LIFEBLOOD

throughout their corridors among the frozen people.

Last of all, she picked up the knife that had been tossed at Joshua's feet, went to the deadwood walkway nearest her mother's cage, and tried to reach out and cut the ropes holding it closed. It was *just* out of reach! Marai made a few more futile attempts, but realized the longer her feet were separated from the ground, the weaker she became. Some of the Lamek warriors next to her started slowly reacting to discovering their weapons had vanished. Marai even noticed the soul eater nearest her starting to turn his head toward her, as if he had spotted her out of the corner of his eye and was turning to get a better look. She had to reconnect to the planet!

Marai jumped off the bridge and caught hold of a tall pike with a skull displayed atop it. It bent and returned her to the bare earth, just as things were starting to move again. They froze in place when she stood upright.

She found herself behind the altar, near the largest cave opening, looking at the back of the man named Sayid. If she could just disarm him, then she would have time to figure out how to bring Joshua out of his time-flow and use his help in saving her mom.

She reached out for Sayid's gun, when suddenly

"Shut up!" Borghaus said.

Louis dropped all the guns in front of him, except one. He held a pistol and pointed it at Hugh.

"You don't realize what you're doing," Hugh said.

"I can't let you stand in the way of me protecting my family!"

"If you pull that trigger…"

A loud report rang out, and Hugh felt the bullet impact his chest. In that moment, Louis had pronounced a verdict on his own head.

Guilty.

He dropped dead before he could pull the trigger again.

mind, and besides, she wasn't entirely convinced he was real anymore.

A sharp pain in her foot as she stepped on a rock alerted her that this line of thinking was taking away her power. She had to relax, but the stress, anger, and doubt made it very difficult. She was losing it!

If she slipped into real time and they noticed her absence, Joshua would be helpless to defend himself against their reaction!

She tried to think of something that would calm her. Almost instinctively, she looked at her mother for comfort. She could see an expression on her face through the bruising.

It was pride.

She was happy to see her daughter again, even if in such dire circumstances. The song that Kit would sing to her as a child when she was afraid of the dark came to Marai's mind. The simple tune melted into her heart.

Marai began to hum it to herself, and was surprised at how quickly she was able to let go of all her anxiety. She regained her grasp on light walking.

She set herself again to the task of disarming all of the Lamek, climbing into the caves and moving

3

On the dark side of the moon above Planet Hope, the Exodus and all of its passengers remained hidden from view. Council Speaker Salman bin Sultan stood at the head of the Council table, with his back to the others.

"Explain to me again how this was supposed to work?" he said. "In words I understand. Why didn't we just launch our EMPs?"

"That's the thing, sir," said Majeed, the Director of Science and Innovation, "it actually is supposed to work like an EMP, without us having to expose our location by launching anything. We turned our nonlinear graviton laser—the thing we generate artificial gravity with—toward the moon's surface, which amplified the moon's magnetic pull on Keppler-186f. The theory is, the electrons on the planet would align one direction and reverse the poles."

"And what will reversing the poles accomplish?" Salman asked, testily. He was upset that he needed to ask. *If they would just assume not everybody is up on their scientific theory...*

even reach her ears. He had wanted her to escape, but she wasn't leaving him there to die, frozen in time. She made a decision to save him.

Marai took off for the nearest Lamek warrior and removed the arrows from his bow and quiver. She broke them over her knee and tossed them into a fire—flames frozen in time—then went to the next man and disarmed him. She continued throughout the village, taking weapons from Lamek and destroying them.

She had to concentrate to keep her mind clear, so that she could continue to move within time at a different rate. If she fell out of her trance even for a moment, the normal passage of time could cause them to react to her disappearance in a dangerous way.

The problem with this was, the Lamek tribe had taken her mother and abused her, using her for bait to lure Marai here—and it had worked. She could feel anger gnawing at her heart, threatening to take her out of her trance. She found that the harder she pushed at it, the stronger it became, and she was probably only moments from slipping.

Marai subconsciously knew she couldn't call for Xrys' help, since words were detrimental to this state of

"Well, it should have worked like an invisible electromagnetic pulse. We never actually got to see what would happen when the poles changed on Earth, but there were many theories, including the destruction of all electronics due to the highly charged electromagnetic field rapidly changing direction. Some also thought pole reversal would result in cataclysmic seismic activity on Earth."

"Like earthquakes and volcanoes and such," Salman said, to show he was following along. "Why haven't we seen any of that happening down there since we fired the pulse?"

"Well, sir, Keppler-186f is a considerably younger planet than Earth was. The single, large continent would seem to indicate that the tectonic plates…err…the plates on which contine…"

"I know what tectonic plates are," Salman snapped.

"Yes, of course. Anyway, the tectonic plates are not as unstable as Earth's, since they're not crashing into one another yet. It seems like our attack didn't affect the planet in that way."

"Then what evidence do we have that anything happened *at all*?"

"I can answer that," Captain Lamb said. Salman turned to face the table, and glared at the Exodus who studies people in far-off jungles?

What if Marai had asked her dad to take her to a movie instead of out for ice cream?

She had a lifetime of regrets, now that she was in this hopeless position. The futility of wishing for impossible change only made the situation more unbearable. What had happened could never be fixed. Time always moved forward, despite anyone's sincerest regrets.

Marai looked up at her mother one last time. Her mother lay at the bottom of the cage, reaching an arm out for Marai through the gnarled wooden bars. Marai felt a deep sorrow well up inside her, pressing on her heart.

She looked over at Joshua, who was still looking at her. He didn't move his unflinching gaze from her, even when Sayid called for his attention.

He held perfectly still.

Too still.

He was sending a message to Marai.

She took two small steps backward, out of her shoes.

Marai emptied her mind and watched as everything around her became still. Sound waves didn't captain's back as he pulled up some images on the screen.

"These are images our moon rover shot of the planet over the course of the detonation. This was the planet before the pulse, and then after." The screen showed darkness on the continents where city lights once blazed. We know it was extensive and crippling damage. Let's go back to the first image. You can see satellites here"—he indicated red circles on the picture—"here, and here, but a full rotation after the pulse, no sign of satellite flares, meaning the electronic mechanisms controlling the solar panels have failed."

"So the waves went all the way through the atmosphere?" Salman asked.

"It would appear so, yes," Captain Lamb answered.

"How long is this blackout supposed to last?" Salman asked.

"We basically sent them back to the stone ages. Everything the aliens used for energy was probably technology based. They shouldn't recover from this for years," Majeed said.

"Can we expect the population to thin out?"

"Hard to say," Captain Lamb said. "We're dealing with an unknown species with unknown technology. They

XVII

"Hope."

Marai saw despair in Joshua's eyes, even as he said the word.

This couldn't be the end! Her mother was only fifteen feet above them! Marai couldn't get *this* close to her just to have it all end so tragically!

Perhaps Joshua had been right. Perhaps all they had were their acts and the natural consequences that arose from them. Perhaps "destiny" was a fool's dream; a sedative for those who believed every story should have a happy ending. Those events that led them to this point might never have come to pass if Marai had made one, tiny, different decision in the past. Where would they be now if Marai had just asked her mom to stay *one more day* in the Tutek village? Where would they be if Marai hadn't gone up the mountain on a fantasy hike, but had stayed in the camp and bonded with her mother instead? What if her mother had never gotten a job as an anthropologist could be prepared to weather an outage like this indefinitely."

Majeed interjected. "In most technology-based societies, the sudden loss of all power creates a communication gap that normally results in chaos."

"Meaning?" Salman asked.

"Meaning, combined with the loss of ability to transport and store food, we should expect some major casualties, regardless of their species."

"Kind of like Earth, when the meteorite destroyed our crops?" Captain Lamb asked.

"I would assume so," Majeed answered.

"How long before we can move?" Salman asked.

"I would give it a year," said Majeed.

"Very well," Salman said. "We've waited this long, we can wait a year more. In the meantime, I'm sending a squad of SF agents down to the planet's surface to find agent Kent Waller and see what has become of the boy."

"You are still worried about Joshua?" Captain Lamb asked. "What harm could he possibly do now?"

Salman wheeled on the captain and looked him fiercely in the eyes. He felt an instant flash of anger, but knew he needed to calm himself in front of everyone. Many in the room didn't know…

To tell you the truth, I'm stranded down here also, since my shuttle was destroyed, so I have nothing better to do than this. I can draw this out as long as I please.

"Tell me, honestly…do you see this ending any other way than with your lifeless body on the ground?"

Joshua cast another glance around the village and made another quick mental assessment.

"No," he said, truthfully.

"Then I really must know: Why is the boy who was heralded for his genius on The Exodus so foolish as to carry out such a poorly-planned rescue attempt?"

He looked at Marai, and answered, "Hope."

"Harm? You misunderstand, captain. I will not have the future of the human race exposed to an unknown, hostile species! We need to find him and bring him back safely!"

In truth, Salman couldn't handle the thought of that kid running free, threatening to undo all he had done, and taking his dark secret with him. Joshua was the last living member of the Darwin Generation, which the Council had genetically created on the ship in case the scientists on board the Exodus were unable to perfect cryogenic freezing. Cryogenic freezing to create a stasis-like sleep had never before been accomplished, but the impending destruction of planet Earth had given them no choice but to launch into space and figure it out during the voyage. The enhanced life-span of the Darwin kids was *only* supposed to come in play if the limited number of cryo-beds proved ineffective, in which case, they became humanity's only hope by surviving over the course of a 490-light-year voyage.

It had been Salman's idea to use the kids as test subjects on the beds. He had justified this to the Council by arguing that the kids lacked the "Earth experience" necessary for a *true* survival of their species, and besides, they didn't *really* represent humanity as a species since their genetic code was changed to eliminate all the to Kent. Joshua looked up and saw Kent step into some torchlight in a cave, smiling. Joshua's heart sank.

"No," Marai breathed from behind him.

"Pick it up," Sayid prompted.

"You don't bring a knife to a gunfight, Sayid." The words came easy now, bursting into bright syllables.

"I'm sorry I didn't have any extra guns; they all seem to have been destroyed," Sayid said. Joshua could see he meant it. His bravado was driving his actions, and apparently, he got a thrill out of killing. "But I've seen you fight, and you're more than capable. Who knows, maybe you'll get lucky and I'll miss?"

"You might miss, but they won't," Joshua said. All of the Lamek warriors were now pointing arrows and javelins at him.

"You might be right, except for one thing: I won't miss. Now pick up the knife."

"Why are you stalling? Why wasn't I dead the moment I stepped into this village?"

"That's not how this works," Sayid said. "The ones without weapons are usually the ones who stall. I have complete confidence that the only way this ends is with you dead. As well as that girl, if she tries to interfere.

weaknesses *Homo Sapiens* had. If they were lost during the first trial of the cryogenic beds, Earth's scientists would still be around to try again, hopefully ensuring humanity's—and Salman's family's—survival.

When the trial had proven successful, a secret plan had been put into play to eliminate the test subjects to make room for the true people of Earth in the beds, since the original plans for the ship only accounted for enough cryogenic beds for as many passengers left Earth on the ship.

The Darwin Generation had been the idea of the head geneticist, a superstitious man who put his faith in a god who failed to show up when Earth was knocked out of orbit by a meteorite, or even save his life when he stood in the way of Salman's plan. If he was honest with himself, Salman had to admit that the Darwin kids had always made him feel uneasy. Maybe it was their strange, light-blue eyes, maybe it was just knowing that they were better equipped to deal with sickness and aging than he, but he had always felt like the outdated model around them. Speaker of The Council and Savior of Humankind, Salman bin Sultan, downgraded to *Humanity 1.0!*

Only Salman and the few in his closest confidence knew how the Darwin Generation had been jettisoned alive from the ship. The rest of the passengers—including troops will fight *for* the Honored Speaker instead of *against* him. We will wipe this planet clean and start over.

"You were foolish to ever take on Salman in the first place," he continued. "Technically, I'm speaking to someone whose death is about 475 years overdue, so he sent me down here to make sure you catch up. I will not disappoint him."

"Lacrimosa dies illa, Qua resurget ex favilla, Judicandus homo reus," Joshua said quietly, forming the words with his hand and seeing the colors of the song in his head. To his surprise, he discovered that if he concentrated on the colors of the words, he didn't need to form them with his hands anymore. All words had pitch, and all pitches to him had a color and shape. He gently pulled away from Marai and took a step forward.

"What did you expect to do, walking in here unarmed?" Sayid said.

"Talk," Joshua said. The color of the single word burned a warm orange.

"I'm disappointed," Sayid said. "I was looking forward to testing my skills against yours. Here," he said, tossing a familiar-looking knife at Joshua's feet. "At least arm yourself with this." It was the knife Joshua had given most now present in the room—had been told the results were successful, and they would be put to sleep along with the test-subjects, only to wake up at the end of the voyage and discover the Darwin Generation "didn't make it" through the sleep. He didn't regret his decision to rid his ship of those *mutants*.

Somehow, this boy Joshua had escaped the cleansing and hid out on the Exodus over the course of about 470 years while they all slept. *What had he been doing all that time? How many other secrets did he know?*

When they had awoken and discovered Joshua, he once again escaped Salman's elite Special Forces and bolted for the planet's surface in an observation pod. He took with him Salman's element of surprise against the planet's inhabitants along with a knowledge of his genocide, and Salman couldn't have that. He felt the anger boiling up again.

"We're done here!" Salman spat. He turned and left the room with his personal guard, Sayid, who was not only his most trusted guard, but a friend.

While they were in the corridor, Sayid spoke to him. "You will need to send a qualified group down to the planet's surface. They are not only going to be dealing with finding the boy, but also with surviving in an unknown environment. You will also need to trust them to return."

"There's my mom!" Marai whispered. "In the cage hanging near the altar."

When he located her, the number of survival scenarios in his head dropped to zero. She had been placed next to Sayid, so he could prevent any attempts to rescue her. There was no way Joshua could see them rescuing her *and* avoiding Sayid's bullets.

Someone was going to die.

The arm Marai was holding started to twitch.

"We can do this!" Marai whispered. "I believe in you!" Joshua couldn't figure out from where she was drawing hope.

They stopped about twenty feet in front of Sayid. The village was eerily silent. Firelight flickered in Sayid's hungry eyes. He spoke:

"Joshua Hawker. I didn't expect you to be so foolish as to come in through the front gate. She *must* have told you these people want you dead!"

Joshua looked around and read the expressions of the villagers as ones rife with anticipation.

"I'm sure you must be wondering what I am doing here," Sayid said. "I'm doing what *you* planned on doing down here; assembling ground troops. Only, my ground

Salman thought for a bit. "You should be the one to lead the group," he said.

"Me?"

"I trust you to do what needs to be done," Salman said.

"And what is that?" Sayid asked.

"End Joshua Hawker. Permanently."

situation he and Marai found themselves in. Along the walls of the cliff were caves and alcoves cut into the rock. They were filled with Lamek warriors, all armed. A few dozen scenarios quickly played themselves out in his mind as possibilities. He looked to his right and left and noticed the village had bridges and walkways connecting stilted houses, also lined with armed Lamek. The survival scenarios whittled down to a half dozen, changing in his mind according to probability and circumstance. There was no plant life within the village walls to conceal themselves behind should they need to. He noticed everything was dead and bone-dry. The shadows cast by the torches might give them small pockets of darkness to hide in temporarily if they had to escape, but that's only if the sun didn't rise first.

His scenarios changed shape as he continued to war-game in his head. This only took fractions of seconds in his mind, and he grimly realized that their odds of survival in this situation were not very high.

Yet, they still advanced forward toward Sayid.

The most important piece of the puzzle had not been placed yet though: Where was Marai's mother, Kit? He didn't even know what she looked like.

4

Hugh stood in front of his bathroom sink, working by candlelight. Years of confrontations such as this last one had taught him to prepare for the worst, and so he stocked surgical supplies at his house. He pulled the bullet from the open wound and dropped it into the trash, then held gauze over it to stanch the trickle of blood. He kept pressure applied to the wound by wrapping his shoulder with a bandage.

Casually, he glanced up and looked at himself in the mirror while he washed his hands. Standing right behind his injured shoulder was his expected visitor.

"I don't see any gray streaks," he said.

"Jack. Somehow I knew you'd be here for this one," Hugh said.

"Did that guy *really* have to die? He was just doing it for his family. Trying to prepare to survive among all the chaos."

"He should have prepared before the need arose. If *everyone* had prepared, we wouldn't *have* chaos."

WOOD/LIFEBLOOD

"The village is just up ahead," she said. "If it would help, you can hold onto my arm."

"I would like that," Joshua said.

They stepped forward together.

The wooden gate to the village opened with an ominous moan as they approached, as if the Lamek were expecting them. Joshua's hunch was right: They believed this was a moment fated to happen. Joshua was determined to use his agency to thwart the outcome they anticipated. Fate would be what *he* made it, and he would use their own superstitions to catch them off-guard.

Unfortunately, a figure emerging from a cave ruined everything Joshua had planned for. The Council Speaker's personal bodyguard, Sayid, stopped in front of an altar, waiting for them. Joshua knew how dangerous Sayid was. He had heard the stories of how he challenged people on Earth to gunfights, just so he could show off his quickness, and now Joshua could see that Sayid wore his pistol visibly on his hip.

What is he doing here? Joshua thought.

Joshua looked all around the village to assess the

"So he deserved to die?" Jack asked.

"I didn't judge him for his lack of preparation," Hugh said. "He had crossed the line of justified action and was attempting to take *my* life."

"He was scared, Hugh."

Throughout his entire life, Jack had always acted as the voice of reason whenever Hugh lashed out. They had met when Hugh was really young, and became inseparable. Indeed, it was Jack's influence in Hugh's life that had led him to become a judge in the first place. But it was Hugh's own ability to determine on the fly the guilt of a person that led him to become *Chief* Judge over the people of Hope. He trusted his own judgment, despite the fact that Jack didn't always agree with him.

"His fear was misdirected," Hugh said. "*I* wasn't the one threatening his family."

"Perhaps not. But you can see how he might have perceived you were when you stood in his way."

"Jack, he was so drunken with fear that he tried to kill me! As a matter-of-fact, I was just about to let him take a few of my supplies home with him when he dropped everything and shot me *with my own gun! I* didn't cause him to try to take a life. But as soon as he did, the scales of justice dropped exactly the amount of one life, so I merely work unless you are in control!"

"I'm… trying!" he said.

"I need you to be strong for me, Joshua! Be strong for my mom! I can't do this without you!" Joshua started to whimper and shake his head.

"Don't tell me you can't! You can!"

Joshua couldn't seem to break free. He wanted *so badly* to pound his stupid head against a tree, just to snap out of it! But Marai held him tightly and wouldn't let go. *What do I need to do to stop this? Why can't I be in control?*

"Everything will be okay," Marai said, calmly.

Joshua felt his muscles unclench. He could move his hand again.

"You can't know that," he said, head still bowed.

"Yes," Marai said, "but I *believe* it. As long as you're with me."

Joshua relaxed and lifted his head. Marai was smiling at him. Perhaps there *was* something to faith. It gave Marai hope, even though she knew they might be walking to their death. Nothing in life was ever sure, but the perspective Marai kept inspired him. Deep down, all he had wanted to hear is that someone believed in a positive outcome, even if it wasn't him.

rebalanced it."

Jack looked at the bloody bullet in the garbage can, pursed his lips and nodded. "So, off to Congo, eh?" he said, changing the subject.

"Yeah. Checking up on a possible extra-terrestrial threat," Hugh said.

"This is about the meteor?"

"Space ship."

"Ooh! Things just got interesting! *Aliens* postponing a potential world war?"

"Or starting it. Whatever you think, it's classified information and I can't talk about it."

Jack laughed. "Like I wouldn't know eventually," he said.

"I find it less and less necessary to talk to you about everything I'm doing," Hugh said.

"Yeah, but you *want* to tell me about this one, admit it."

"Maybe a little." Hugh resigned himself to spilling Top Secrets to his best friend again. "It seems the President believes there's some sort of alien scouting party down in Congo, near Montsacre. I'm to go down there and judge them."

"What does he think they're here to do?"

"He thinks the main ship is hidden behind the

XVI

As they spotted the light of the village fires lighting up the cliff-side in the distance, Joshua's hands became uncontrollable. His fingers flew about in a frenzy near his head, and he couldn't seem to stop it, no matter how hard he tried.

"Marai…Marai…Marai," he said.

She stopped walking and turned to face him. "Are you anxious, Joshua?" All he could do was nod. His fingers wouldn't work well enough to form the words he wanted to say.

She gently pulled his hands down to his sides, and tried to get him to look at her. "Find a way to form the words, Joshua." His hands still didn't seem to want to cooperate. She held them down firmly as he tried to bring them back up.

"Joshua? Look at me!" She ducked her head down so she could make eye contact with him. "Your plan won't moon, and this is just a forward party sizing us up for invasion."

"Do you think they'll be found guilty?" Jack asked.

"I can't be sure of that until I face them in person."

"If this is real, you could potentially prevent our annihilation."

"How so?"

Jack looked him directly in the eyes with a solemn expression on his face. "Well, Jack, guilty or not, sometimes it's a good thing to shoot the messenger."

"You know I can't..."

"Who you talking to, boss?" an obnoxious voice called from the doorway behind him.

"None of your concern, Tai," Hugh shouted over his shoulder. He was smart enough not to run, but not smart enough to leave Hugh alone when he asked to be.

"You have an imaginary friend?" Tai asked.

Hugh looked back in the mirror and saw Jack was gone.

forward and hugged Joshua. He felt uncomfortable with her being so close. He couldn't quite bring himself to put his arms around her, even though he wanted to. Marai was very attractive, but he knew this was just his emotions clouding his understanding of her intent.

"Thank you, Joshua," she said.

He patted her on the back and then she separated from him.

"When we get to the village, we need to stay out of sight," Marai said. "The soul eaters will spot us if they have reason to look. Hopefully our coming is still a surprise to them."

Joshua made a connection in his mind.

"You say these are pretty fervent believers in fate?" Joshua asked.

"Yes."

"Then I suggest we go a different route."

5

Hugh had a long journey ahead of him, and no motorized vehicle in which to make it. The feeling in his gut told him this event was larger than just an outage, and that he might not be seeing many of his material possessions again. He was fine with that. He had spent his entire life starting over from scratch.

He lit his acetylene torch and started cutting the exterior off his car. Once it was stripped down to the frame, he set to work removing the engine and transmission with the chain lift in his garage. He removed anything that was not necessary to his cause. When he was finished, all that was left on the frame were the seats and steering wheel. He jerry-rigged a harness from leather straps and hitched up the now-lighter car frame to his horses. The sky was starting to lighten when he finally loaded up his supplies and told Tai and Borghaus to get into his makeshift wagon. Tai, of course, hopped into the don't know what you planned to do when you got here, but maybe you should just go about trying to make that happen instead of helping me chase some ancient 'prophecy.' You have had a terrible, tragic life, and the last thing you need is me adding more trouble. You should stay here with your ship. All I want to do is go save my mom or die trying." Her eyes glistened with moisture.

"Marai, I never had any intention of letting you go alone."

"Yeah, but maybe you should. This is my problem, not yours."

"Marai… I'm sorry about what I said earlier about having no friends. Ever since I have been here, you have been a loyal friend to me. It's because of you that I'm alive today."

"It's also because of me that you almost died," Marai said.

"The only thing you did wrong was try to save my life after the crash," Joshua said. "Who knows, maybe if you did nothing, I might have died from head trauma. My point is, you never left me to die, even though your mom's life was in jeopardy. It's my turn to return the favor."

Marai sniffed and nodded. Then she lunged

front seat.

"Sit in the back!" Hugh barked as he carried the last box.

"Why?" Tai argued. "You got room!"

"I don't want to spend weeks listening to you complain." Hugh returned. "In the back!"

Tai grumbled, but did as he was told. Borghaus didn't look too pleased to be sitting next to his noisy travel companion. Hugh set the box in the vacated front seat, sat in the driver's seat, and slapped the reins on the horses' backs. They started off down the road.

A few houses down, Hugh steered the horses into a driveway.

"Where we going now?" Tai asked. Hugh felt too tired and annoyed to explain himself. He stopped the horses near the front door and got out, retrieving the box in the front seat. He scrawled a note and placed it on the box.

Dear Janet,

I am so sorry to tell you, but your husband has died. He was trying to get food and supplies for you and your family, but he turned a gun on me and I had to protect myself. Inside this box are the supplies he had retrieved. I want you to take your family

XV

A few days had passed, and Kent still hadn't returned. Marai kept insisting that they wait a little longer, but Joshua doubted Kent ever had any intention to help them. He had probably just returned to his camp instead of risk his life to help them. At least he wasn't still trying to kill or capture Joshua anymore.

As far as he knew.

When the sun began descending toward evening, Marai came to him wearing concern on her face. She hadn't been the same since their earlier conversation.

"I wonder if they caught him," Marai said. "He might even be dead by now."

"I don't know," Joshua said. "Should we go now, before it's too dark to see the trail?"

Marai hesitated. "Joshua, I've been thinking…"

"Yeah?"

"I'm sorry to have dragged you into all of this. I

and move into my house. I will not be there anymore. There is plenty there for you, as well as whatever is in the garden. I feel things are going to get worse, but you should be safer there. I am so sorry about your loss.

You will find Louis resting peacefully underneath my willow tree. Take care of yourselves.

-Hugh Winters

Hugh hurt for her, but couldn't be upset about his actions. He knew he was just in his judgment, otherwise the man, Louis, wouldn't have dropped dead the moment he decided to steal Hugh's life. The balance scales were tipped back to normal, and even though Louis didn't succeed in taking Hugh's life, he took up a weapon and *attempted* to, and that was enough to forfeit his own claim to life.

Balance.

Hugh knew more than anyone where that balance needed to be. After all his years of interacting with the human race, Hugh seemed to be able to see things in people's actions beyond what was visible to the naked eye. He could tell when a killing was justified even without about someone they had lost, and she would feel slightly guilty for going about her busy life, going days and weeks without remembering him. And now, even the *possibility* that she might not actually see him again stabbed at her heart. She didn't want it to be true, but the harder she wished, the more she thought about the possibility that it was her desperation that drove her visions.

She had to know.

Marai lay down on the cool ground, closed her eyes, and took in deep breaths. She listened to the forest around her and tried to let go of her physical senses. After a few minutes of nothing happening, she realized she was still very corporeal. Had she just been dreaming the hyper-realistic dreams of a schizophrenic each time? She called out to Xrys in her mind.

Xrys? Xrys?

…No answer.

Xrys, I need to know if you are real, or if I am just imagining you. …Still no answer.

Xrys… please!

After an hour of silence, she realized she was alone.

Marai rolled onto her face and began to weep.

having witnessed the crime. The air felt heavier when someone was taken before their appointed time. Only by the slightest touch on his skin, but heavier, nonetheless. It was as if with their dying breath they were crying out for justice, and Hugh could feel it. Those who died trying to take another's life without justification had no such righteous cause, and they knew it.

But in order for him to rebalance the scale, Hugh had to stop a person in the act of trying to take a life. He had encountered many killers in his quest for righteousness, but was powerless to pass judgment until they took up arms. Of course, he could always just shoot them with the gun he carried, but he wanted to be *sure* of his actions, and often could prompt someone quick to kill to make an attempt on him when confronted. That made the job so much less messy. He didn't delight in doing it, but he certainly was justified in every case.

Even though Hugh reassured himself of his actions, that didn't make this last situation any easier. Louis had walked a fine line between cold-blooded murder and self-defense. He had been so frightened by his current situation that he feared for his own life, and even though he was in no danger of losing his life to Hugh, he had no

She admitted to herself that since that tragic event, she had been searching for him. Maybe this was all just an invention of her subconscious mind longing to see him again.

And how had that worked out?

She hadn't ever seen her father; she just saw these people who had a convenient way of explaining why she couldn't see him. People nobody else saw. It was hard to think that her experiences might be fabricated. It had all seemed so real. But now that doubts started to settle in, Marai could see how Joshua's perspective could be all-the-more possible.

And if Joshua was right about about Xrys being a fabrication, that would mean everything she believed (or hoped?) about life after death was wrong. It would mean there wasn't a soul that lived on after death. It would mean the moment her father had died, he ceased to exist in any form, except for in her memory of him.

If that was the way things were, then she cursed herself for not thinking about him more often, so she could preserve those precious memories of him throughout the remainder of her short life. She had always heard people claim there wasn't a day they didn't think way of knowing that. To him, Hugh stood in the way of his family's very survival.

Still…

Louis had made a choice, and he knew it was wrong the moment he made it. Everything from the slight widening of his eyes to his hand not releasing its tension as the gunshot rang out told Hugh he had chosen against reason.

To what sad end?

Hugh looked up and saw a young girl looking at him through the curtains of an upstairs room. She smiled and waved. Hugh waved back, and then stood and turned to go to the car. He stepped in and sighed deeply before snapping the reins.

"You crying, boss?" Tai asked.

"Shut up," Hugh replied.

XIV

Marai walked by the river on her own. She just had to get away so she could process all the things that were said. She still remembered her experiences with Xrys vividly, and was pretty sure they had happened the way she had witnessed them, but in the back of her mind was a small nagging doubt.

What if he's right? If I was crazy, would I know it?

Even her own mother had said she had walked up the Sacred Mountain alone. She knew her mother was pretty skeptical when it came to spiritual matters, and Marai hadn't been too keen to share her experiences with her mom. Or anyone, really, until this point. Perhaps this was because she was afraid of being told the truth? Of having her comfortable worldview challenged? The things Joshua said to her were harsh, but if she really *was* crazy, he was only trying to awaken her to reality.

It had started with her father's untimely murder.

6

Sayid had always known where he needed to be. His whole life on Earth had been spent in the shadow of power. From an early age, he had believed Salman bin Sultan would be a powerful man someday, and while Sayid didn't aspire to such power, he knew the benefits of having access to it. He made sure Salman knew his primary school friend was also his most loyal. Sayid also knew the benefits of operating from the shadows in case an assassin someday decided he didn't like the current ruling party.

Sayid had a way of suggesting things that made Salman think he had come up with the idea himself, and he could use this to help Salman achieve greatness. Salman was royalty, after all. His uncle was the most powerful man in the Middle East. And even though Salman was not in line for the throne, Sayid knew better.

Because he would *make* it better.

Sayid followed Salman to the United States so

was frozen in time. Whereas, when you do it, you look like you're speeding up; to the point it looks like you disappear to the outside observer, but to you, time looks frozen."

"It's the same thing, except I didn't have to invent ghosts to help me understand what's happening," he said. "This is all within the realms of human ability and nothing more.

"We're on our own out here, Marai."

they could both earn degrees at a prestigious ivy-league school and make connections with people who would someday become world leaders. Salman's family status had even earned many trips to the White House.

After earning their degrees, they worked in different embassies, making even more connections with European leaders. Sayid only suggested Salman build a network of influence among people he was sure would amount to more than "just" a leader.

When they were back home, people of influence started mysteriously dying of natural causes, or were even put to death following damning evidence of treason against the King. Salman's hands were clean of any wrongdoing, but only because Sayid's were not. Sayid dared not even tell the person he did this for, so Salman would not accidentally expose his plot. And it had worked! Salman found himself next-in-line for the kingdom upon the King's death.

This was easy enough to accomplish when the world erupted in chaos. Sayid knew nobody would care if the King was found with a large bullet hole in his chest, when they were so concerned with their own, immediate survival. Once the fighting and rioting had died down, they

"Do you really want me to answer that question?"

"Yes, I do," Marai said, crossing her arms.

"Because it might shake your faith," he said.

"Lay it on me," she said. "Let's hear what science has to say about this."

"I'd rather show you," Joshua said. "Come over here and stand by me." Marai walked over to him, curious how he was going to explain away what she had done.

"I want you to hold my hand and empty your mind of any words. Just focus on the images in your field of view." Marai took his hand and emptied her mind. The jungle went suddenly dark, and Marai saw the reflection of the moon traveling across the pool at a rapid pace. The sky started to lighten and the sun appeared over the trees and then stopped. Joshua let go of her hand.

"Look around you," Joshua said. "It's tomorrow.

"I just did what you did, except in the other direction. We're both interrupting the processes of timekeeping in the left hemispheres of our brains in order to perceive the passage of time at different rates. Do you remember how I told you I went into stasis to travel through a 490-light-year voyage? This is how I did it. If you were to see me when I did it, it would just look like I looked to a leader to save them from certain doom, and didn't question how Salman had gotten there. And to them, he *was* a great leader. Sayid had groomed him as such.

Salman had believed he, of himself, was the great leader that had put himself in the prime position of Council Speaker, the highest authority of those who would put together a plan to escape Earth, but the notion of forming a council to create a "democracy" was Sayid's idea, subtly suggested to Salman. Only a democracy where everyone operated under the illusion that they had an equal say would work among the most powerful, egotistical people on Earth. These were they who could contribute enough money or resources to build and buy passage on the Exodus. A speaker needed to be appointed to speak in behalf of the council, and Sayid used this as a deceptive way of granting Salman just a little non-threatening power over the council. In their minds, a "speaker" was little more than a "messenger,"—and possibly even *beneath* a seated member—but Sayid knew the one with the voice would be viewed by the *people* as the one with the power.

Sure, these secret councils had existed long before the meteor ever appeared in the sky, but when it struck,

Marai just stood there with her hands hanging at her sides.

"You have tried so hard to make sense of everything after your dad died, that you have invented a world where people still exist after they die," Joshua said. "They don't. Believe me, I have looked, and I have lost *everyone*."

Marai shook her head. "Come outside," she said. "I have to show you something."

She climbed down from the pod and stood on the rainforest floor next to the pool, waiting as Joshua slowly made his way down the ladder. When he reached the bottom, Marai faced Joshua and removed her shoes. She emptied her mind, and walked to a different spot. Then she came out of her trance. Joshua looked surprised.

"I was taught to do something outside of the understanding of science by a person you claim isn't real. To you, it looked like I disappeared and then reappeared in a different spot, but I was just connecting to the spirit of the planet and walking at a normal speed. Now you have experienced it as well, and you have no reason to disbelieve me. Do you have an explanation for this that fits within your understanding of what's 'real?'"

the chaos threatened to destroy their connections and strand Salman and his lowly bodyguard, Whatshisname, on a dying planet. Sayid prompted Salman to move quickly to bring them all together with the world's leading scientific minds in their home country in an "altruistic attempt to save humankind." Altruism only went so far as one's own family and friends, though, which was fine by Sayid. He was included in that group. The unfortunate designers and builders of the great Exodus were given no such option. They were too valuable to leave behind, but not valuable enough to make room for their families at the expense of the elites' families.

Besides his AK-47, Sayid always kept a .45 Colt Single Action Army revolver in a holster at his side. During his time in America, he had grown an affinity for western films, and had always wanted to be the quickest draw. He had grown fond of the Colt revolver because of the ease of manually striking the taller hammer with his free hand for a faster fire. Indeed, with enough practice, he could shoot faster than someone with a semi-automatic handgun. The trade-off of using a revolver instead of a handgun with a magazine was a limited round capacity, but he had reasoned that if he couldn't make his deadly point the wall. One of his hands started writing.

"It's not about whether *you're* real or not, it's about the people you see that *nobody else can.*" Joshua said. "On this planet, do you diagnose for schizophrenia? It's the disease where people see an alternate reality."

"Yes, we have a disease like that."

"Schizophrenics believe people are real who are *absolutely not*; but to them, it's concrete truth that they *are.*"

"But are those imaginary people *really* real?" Marai responded.

"To *them*, yes!" Joshua said.

"Then why do we diagnose it as a disease and try to cure them if it's okay for everyone to have an alternate view of what's real?"

"I'm not saying it should be acceptable, it's just the way it is. Think about what we're talking about, here; the *perception* of reality. Faulty brain wiring or not, reality and truth are as varied as there are individuals. *Everyone* lives by a different truth."

Marai realized something: "Do you believe *I* have schizophrenia?"

"If you did, would you know it? You see people nobody else does. That's your reality."

in six tries, he was wasting bullets anyway.

He used hollow-point bullets, so even if he was slightly off in his aim, the bullet would do enough damage to make up the difference. After years of perfecting his art, he finally had opportunities to show off his skills. Any individuals he suspected of plotting to rise up and overthrow the Council during the construction of the ship were dropped with a cricket-ball-sized exit wound through their back. He had always faced the traitors so they would know who killed them and could perhaps marvel at his quickness as their life quickly slipped away. It was always so much more satisfying if they were armed. If he confronted a group of conspirators, he found it never took more than six bullets to dissuade them from any ill intentions. The rest he finished off with the AK, just because they took part.

All this he did without Salman having a clue. Salman still believed he was in his position of influence on his own merits, but always there had been an operative in his shadow, secretly paving the way before him.

Today, Sayid was leaving Salman's side. After years of being on this ship, Sayid was ready to feel the earth beneath his feet once again, alien planet or not. It

"Faith has nothing to do with science!" Joshua shouted. His sudden change of demeanor caught Marai by surprise. He seemed angry. "How can you study something nobody can see?!"

"But I *can* see," Marai said, touching him on the shoulder. He seemed to calm down with the human contact. "I'm somebody."

He started to shake his head. "I don't believe you," Joshua said. "At least I don't believe you are interpreting events correctly."

Now it was Marai's turn to be upset. "Is that what this all boils down to? My experiences are not yours so they *can't* be real? There's no way you can experience everything personally, so how can you know what is true or not?"

"I don't have to. Truth is relative to the individual," he said.

Marai stood up out of the chair she had been sitting in. "That is the stupidest, most egocentric thing I've ever heard! No matter how convinced you were that I'm not real, I would *still* exist!" She slapped him across the face and said, "Did that feel *real* to you?"

He covered his head and started pacing closer to

was time to jump ship, literally.

He put together a team that he believed would give him the best chance of success, not to mention survival. Since he knew Kent was one of the American mercenaries Salman had hired to do dirty work on Earth, he would bring along one of Kent's squad members, Donny "The Grouch" Groutage. A handful of the Special Forces agents on the ship were made up of a group of these mercenaries. They were unprincipled men, who only placed value in the money their skills could earn. Many of them had served in elite forces of the American military in wartime, and having knowledge of the territory and culture of the Middle East, had decided to become "soldiers of fortune" after they were discharged. Groutage was a former Navy Seal, and seemed to have no ties to anyone outside of his squad of mercs.

Also coming along was Li Chaoxiang, the resident martial-arts expert on The Exodus. Sayid had seen the surveillance footage of Joshua cutting a swath through SF agents as he made his escape through the hangar, and wanted someone with him in case Joshua somehow engaged them in hand-to-hand combat. What the 15-year-old boy had done to full-grown, combat-trained men was

Marai told him her story, starting from when her father died. She told him of how she had come to the jungle with her mother while her mom studied the Tutek, how they had been hunted by men with no eyes, how she met Xrys and learned from him how to light walk and spirit walk. She told him about the cave, where the prophecy of her meeting with Joshua had been etched in stone millennia before. Last of all, she told how the village had been attacked when her mother was away, and how she had to escape from Lamek soul eaters. Her story also ended where theirs began.

Joshua stood in silence, slowly patting his bowed head with both hands.

Marai was worried about him. "Joshua, are you okay?"

"I'm just trying to make sense of it," Joshua said. "I think it's all a pretty good story, but I'm having trouble making it fit into my understanding of the universe."

"It happened, Joshua. Just the way I described it."

"I'm sure it might *seem* that way to you," Joshua said. "But, logically, it just doesn't connect to any of the observable universe."

"That's where faith comes in," Marai said.

impressive, but nothing compared to what Sayid had seen Li do. Li could drop a man twice his size just by grabbing his hand in a certain way. It was a pity Li had not had the chance to encounter Joshua during his escape.

Sayid also brought along two people with knowledge of biology and ecology, so that they could ensure their safety when they reached the planet's surface. One was a Kenyan man who had been researching and publishing world-renowned studies on possible life-systems on Mars, and just happened to be in Riyadh when the meteorite struck. He had not been allowed to return home to Kenya, but his misfortune would hopefully yield positive results for Sayid in an unknown clime. His name was too complicated for everyone to pronounce, so they all just called him "Bo."

The other was a female ecologist named Hannah McCall. She had been forced onto The Exodus against her will, plucked from a nearby university where she had been doing graduate research. She had graduated at the top of her class in her undergraduate studies, and was an emerging mind in the field of ecology. She had been pregnant when she was brought onto the Exodus project, and had lost the baby during childbirth. Her demeanor was

"It was still *my* decision to wave my hand."

Marai agreed with him, but she didn't see the point in arguing about it. This conversation was obviously agitating Joshua. But apparently, he wasn't done.

"When I get to the end of my life, the only satisfaction I'll take is in knowing I made my own choices."

"What happens after you die if those choices are poor? Can you live with yourself then?" Marai asked.

Joshua looked over at her out of the corner of his eye. "I heard you having a conversation with nobody the other morning."

Marai knew where this was headed, so she just told him the truth: "I was speaking with my friend, Xrys. He died right before I met you."

"You were speaking with a spirit?" Joshua asked. "Why couldn't I see him?"

"I could only *hear* him," Marai corrected.

"But you claim you were hearing an audible voice that I couldn't hear?"

"Yes," Marai said. "But… I can see him, too, when I spirit walk."

"Spirit walk?"

usually sullen, which Sayid found annoying. She could have just stayed on Earth and burned with the rest of humanity!

The five of them prepared a pod with enough supplies to last two months. Sayid did not expect to take that long locating the boy, but he wanted to come prepared, just in case.

"What exactly is this mission all about?" Bo asked as they loaded crates into the observation pod.

"That's classified," Groutage replied.

"It must have something to do with studying the conditions on the planet, otherwise they wouldn't be bringing us," Hannah said in answer to Bo's question.

"But why wouldn't we be sending down whole teams of scientists? Why just the five of us, only two of whom are scientists?" Bo asked.

"Consider us the forward party, so to speak," Sayid said. "I just need you to accompany us to ensure our biological safety while we search for one of our own."

"Someone made it down to the surface?" Bo asked. He set down the crate he was carrying and approached Sayid. "Who was it?"

"Agent Groutage was right; you do not need to concern yourself with the details. We will do our job as

Joshua said. He waved his arm in the air. "There. I've just changed the outcome of my life. I made a decision to wave my hand just now and *did it*, and that just set me down an entirely different path than I would have ended up on had I not decided to wave my hand. The point is, it was *my* decision to do it, and I did."

"I agree that you have the freedom to choose. I just believe it all fits within a certain framework, is all," Marai said.

"But, see… that 'framework' would imply I didn't have any choice at all! That it wasn't *really* my decision to wave my arm and screw up my future, but that some higher power caused me to do that so I would fit into some plan."

"Maybe the higher power just knew you would make that decision and shaped creation to accommodate it, even if it was just letting the natural consequences teach you."

"What, you mean, like, fixing every bad mistake I've made? Because I think my life would be a lot easier if I had made some different choices."

"Maybe life isn't only about living easy."

Joshua got up and started pacing the shuttle floor.

long as you do yours."

"So stop asking questions and load that crate," Groutage said.

Bo sighed, picked up the crate, and disappeared into the dark interior of the pod. Hannah picked up her crate and followed him, no doubt to talk out of earshot of Sayid. He took the opportunity to do the same.

"Grouch, Li," he said in a hushed tone, keeping his eyes on the pod opening.

"Yes, sir?" they said in near unison, coming close in response to his nonverbal cues.

"Have you been briefed on every aspect of this mission?"

"Find Kent Waller and bring him back," Li said.

"That's not everything," Groutage said. "We need to find the boy Joshua and kill him."

It grated at Sayid that Groutage was so desperate to seem important and in-the-know that he couldn't wait for his superior officer to do the briefing.

"Easier said than done, eh Grouch?" Sayid said. He had seen footage of this 6-foot-4 man being dropped by Joshua with a pinch to the thigh as he made his escape through the hangar, and he knew this comment would

"Sometimes, it's okay to just accept things we don't understand," Marai said.

"That goes against my nature. I am *always* trying to find out the mechanisms that put anomalies into place. There's always been a sound explanation for everything."

"Why not just make it easier on yourself and have faith that things will operate as they were created to do? Then just accept your purpose in that plan."

"See, that's where I get hung up," Joshua said. "I'm not sure there *is* a specific plan for my life."

"Then how do you explain the events that brought us together?"

"It's easy to look back on your life and start to map out events as if they were coordinated to bring you to a certain point. But what if I had made *one tiny decision* differently during that same life and had arrived at a completely different point? Would *that* then be the way it was 'fated' to happen? There's an infinite amount of decisions in life with an infinite amount of different outcomes! Are each of those paths 'meant' to be, or are they just the natural outcomes of my decisions?"

"But, you ended up *here*," Marai said.

"With autism and no living parents or friends,"

sting Grouch's ego.

"That little brat isn't going to get close enough to touch me this time!" Groutage said, tapping his rifle as if to make a point.

Good. Sayid wanted him to keep his anger fresh, so that he would stay on-task when they reached planet-side.

"They are not to know about Joshua Hawker," Sayid said, indicating with a gesture of his head the other two in the pod.

"Why, sir?" Li asked.

"Technically, the boy wasn't supposed to be alive in the first place."

"Wasn't *supposed* to be alive?" Li asked. "I thought the Darwin Generation didn't survive the cryogenic freezing because of some genetic something-or-other."

"They were jettisoned like space trash," Groutage said with a smug look on his face. Sayid wanted to punch him for being so casual with privileged information. He must have been one of the few SF agents brought in to perform the deed, while Li was left asleep.

"So you're telling me that Kent was not the 'rogue agent' who stole a ship and escaped to the planet, but it's this kid, Joshua?" Li asked.

XIII

While they waited, Marai conversed with Joshua. They never really had been given a chance to get to know one another, and now that Joshua was verbal again, she was fascinated to learn his story. He told her more of his origin, how he didn't really have a traditional birth, but instead was created to be able to live out a longer life with others in his generation. He told her of his ability to make connections at a really young age, and how he used to "draw" songs in bright colors. He told her the story of when his generation had been discarded when it was discovered they would not be necessary, and how he had escaped and survived, completely alone, over the course of a 490-year voyage. Then he told of his escape from The Exodus, and how a series of strange events, including landmarks in the ground, had brought him to meet her.

"I don't understand it all," Joshua said, "but I believe there's a rational explanation for it."

"Yes," Sayid confirmed. "But we spread the story of Kent escaping to quell the rumors of a survivor."

"So we get the dirty job of cleaning up after the Speaker's messes," Groutage chuckled. Before he could even blink, Sayid had a pistol drawn and pointed at the empty space between Groutage's eyebrows.

"You will speak with respect about the Honored Speaker of the Council!" Sayid hissed. The jovial expression left Groutage's face as he realized Sayid was being dead serious. He slowly raised his hands as he stared at the gun pointed in his face.

"I'm sorry, sir," Groutage said. "I meant no disrespect."

Sayid flirted with the idea of ending his life right here and choosing someone more tolerable to take down in his spot, but the bead of sweat running down Groutage's temple assured Sayid he had learned his lesson and wouldn't be so flippant from here on. He was like a dog, who only needed to know who the alpha male was.

Just then, Sayid heard someone to his right and looked over to see Hannah and Bo looking on with shock.

"Time to fly," Sayid said as he holstered his pistol. Then into a radio he said, "Fire."

"Tell me, woman. Are you frightened?"

She didn't answer, but she knew her panicked whimpers betrayed her.

"Does this not look like control to you?" he said. "I cause you to fear, and that makes me more powerful than you. You are weak. Kindness cannot save you."

The man stood, threw beans at her, and started down the walkway. "You should pray to your god to deliver you so you can see just how "weak" I am when I finally kill you. You will watch your daughter die, and I will be right here next to you when the time comes. My blade will then taste your blood."

So Kit prayed, hoping there was a god to hear her plea.

7

A blinding burst of light suddenly filled the sky, lighting up everything around Hugh's cart as if it were daytime. He immediately shielded his eyes and looked behind him through the slits between his fingers. A bright mushroom-shaped cloud was ominously growing skyward where the city of Capital had stood, now forty to fifty miles behind him. All of the people in the city who had been fighting to survive were gone in an instant, Hugh knew. Along with them, some of the oldest buildings on planet Hope, as well as all the rich history of their people preserved meticulously in writing, stored in the vaults and shelves of the First Library.

"All them people…" Tai said as he looked on in shock.

In his heart, Hugh mourned more for the loss of the records than he did for the people. Generations came and went, but they lived on through words. Their society

"And what good does keeping me alive do?"

"There is a strong bond between a mother and her child," he said. "She will be drawn to you."

"I would threaten to kill you all if you harm her, but I think you actually *desire* death."

The man smiled. "Not all of us," he said. "There are some far too weak to embrace the paths of The Destroyer. It takes strength to live like this. If no man can stand up to us, all that is theirs is ours by right, including his life. We take what we want, when we want it, and *force* Creation to serve us."

"You consider kindness and patience to be a weakness, but it takes far more strength to be kind to those you disagree with, or to have to wait or work to get what you want fairly," Kit said.

"And then you are killed by a stronger man."

"With no control over himself."

Without warning, he jabbed his hand through the cage and grabbed her hair, pulling her head into the bars. He brought his face close to hers. She could smell the stench of rotting death on his breath. She struggled to pull free from his grip, but couldn't do anything in her weakened state.

had been built around preserving their language through records-keeping, and now it was all destroyed. Whether this was the work of some of the enemies of the state or the visitors, Hugh couldn't guess. He had never seen an explosion so big. He definitely had nothing to go back for now. He saw the trees behind him bowing in submission to such a powerful force and he quickly turned to protect his face against the coming shockwave.

A forceful wind blew him forward in his seat and he felt his makeshift cart turn sideways in the road. The horses whinnied and had to take side steps just to stay upright. As quickly as the wind came, it departed, leaving a strange calm in the air. Hugh glanced back again and saw the stars in the night sky being blotted out by a cloud of ash. He righted his horses in their path and increased their pace down the road.

When they came to an old highway leading off in another direction, Hugh reigned his horses into a turn.

"Why we going on this road?" Tai asked.

"I think it's best if I avoid any population centers on the way down," Hugh said. "I have a feeling this wasn't an isolated attack."

"That explosion was far too big to be caused by

Ka'ar and had a red-hot skewer stabbed into their eyes. They then had their eyelids sewn shut and their faces painted white. It was the making of the monsters that had sought her daughter's life since the day they had arrived.

The strangest ritual she saw, though, was where the captive man offered on the altar was spared and the priest took his own life instead. The Lamek worshipped death so much that they brought it upon themselves.

Why didn't they just kill her? Kit wished she could end her miserable captivity if it meant her daughter would stay far away from this place. Or better yet, the Lamek could all just take their own lives and rid Hope of their presence if they loved death so much!

A young skull-faced man walked by on the suspended rope bridge next to her cage and squatted down to be close to her. "I have brought you food," he said.

"Another handful of dried beans?" Kit said.

"We do not want you dead, but that does not mean you must be so alive."

"If you know where she is, why have you not gone after her?" Kit asked.

"We are waiting for her to come here, where our magic is strong."

anything we have on this planet," the usually quiet Borghaus interjected. Hugh knew he would have information about weapons technology, coming from the position he did. He prodded him to continue:

"Go on."

"There were theories about how to harness the power of the atom in order to create a massive bomb capable of wiping out an entire city," Borghaus said.

"You didn't sell any of this information, did you?" Hugh asked.

"I didn't dare," Borghaus answered. "I knew they would use this information to kill millions of people. All I wanted was money."

"What did you do with that research when you left?" Hugh asked.

"I destroyed it. No point in *anyone* wielding that type of power."

"So chances are this is an attack from our otherworldly visitors?"

"Would seem so," Borghaus nodded. They moved on in silence for some time.

"Yeah, keep out the big cities, boss," Tai said.

XII

In her malnourished state, Kit lost track of time. How long had she been locked in a cage? Days? *Weeks?* Kit had realized how solitary confinement could drive a person crazy, and now here she was, bordering on the brink of insanity.

She wasn't sure if some of the atrocities she witnessed were the effects of a frenzied mind or reality. Perhaps this was because she didn't want to believe that such acts were humanly possible. It made her wonder how human beings could ever bring themselves to such a base state. The Lamek had sacrificed a few people on their blood-stained altar and dripped the blood onto unearthed bones, then blew on a large horn which echoed through the jungle, frightening off a flock of birds in a tree just outside the wall. She watched them cannibalize the remains, and then throw their bones into a bonfire. She had seen a ritual where men knelt before the High Priest

Hugh rode for a few weeks along the back roads, stopping to sleep every night and let his horses rest. They stayed far enough away from the cities that they didn't witness any more explosions. They would see the occasional traveler on the road, but normally there was no conversation passed between them. They kept their heads down and marched onto their destinations, normally with hasty packs thrown over their backs. There were others who would spot them a long way off and run into the bushes or trees next to the road to hide from Hugh. He made sure to keep a rifle leaning on the seat next to him, more for their protection than his. The sight of armed traveler might dissuade them from making any hasty decisions that would bring Hugh's judgment upon them.

After a while, the climate began to grow more humid, and the occasional palm tree would spring up from the ground. Hugh pulled his horses to the side of the road on a hilltop and unslung his rifle to look through the scope.

"What you looking for?" Tai asked. *Always a question needing answered with him.*

city of "Kent" had a nice, Earthy ring to it.

Whatever the mission, he knew his brightly-colored parachute was a good signal for anyone flying over to see. If he went back to camp, he was bound to be discovered sooner-or-later.

On the other hand, he wouldn't be much help to Marai in her quest to find her mother. He liked Marai, and even liked Joshua slightly more than he had before, but maybe that was just because he saw a bit of Andrew in Joshua and felt remorse for leaving him behind. Whatever the case, Kent knew he was no hero, and maybe doing something totally against his will to survive would redeem him.

Who was he kidding? One selfless act couldn't erase a lifetime of atrocities and bad decisions.

Could it?

As he stood there thinking, a ship suddenly passed overhead, flying in the direction of his camp. Kent made his decision.

He set his jaw and started down the path.

"'That," Hugh said pointing. He didn't hand over his rifle to Tai, for obvious reasons. Far off on the horizon was Montsacre, the destination Hugh had set off for a lifetime ago. The mountain was the tallest peak on the planet by many tens of thousands of feet, so its miniscule stature on the horizon told Hugh they still had many miles to go yet. "The Sacred Mountain," Hugh said, in case Tai asked.

"I am from there!" Tai informed everyone.

"Why do you think I brought you along?" Hugh replied.

"Because I am charming?" Tai asked.

"Nope."

"So you have something pretty to see next to this ugly one?" Tai said, indicating Borghaus. Borghaus took a swipe at him, which he deftly dodged, laughing.

"You're here to help me with the natives," Hugh said.

"O-oh, you won't like my family," Tai said. "They *way* uglier than Borghaus! Some of them sew they eyes shut!"

back so they could make plans. Oh, and all without being caught and killed by bloodthirsty cannibals. *Sounded simple.*

Down the trail to his left was his camp that he had just started settling into. He had made a pretty good treehouse, and had used his bright parachute as a covering and a signal to anyone from the ship flying over. In his heart, he still hoped he would be rescued and brought back to the ship. He wondered if his friend Grouch would try to convince someone to send out a search party for him. After years of saving each others' skins, he couldn't imagine Grouch leaving his brother-in-arms behind. He was the closest thing to family Kent had.

Regardless, Joshua was right about them sending a search party, although knowing The Speaker, he probably sent his lap-dog Sayid after Joshua on a search-and-destroy mission rather than any attempt to rescue Kent. They knew Kent was down here, because he had told Sayid of his plan over the radio when he went to hide himself in Joshua's pod. While they had been actively searching for Joshua in the mechanical workings of the ship, Kent had gone with his hunch that this was where the boy had been headed. Sayid told him that if he was right, he would be rewarded with a settlement of his own after the purge. The

8

A few hours after the first rounds of nukes were launched, Sayid piloted the observation pod down in a trajectory punched into the navigation computer, tracing the path which Joshua's had taken weeks before. He didn't know how far the boy could have gotten by now, but he did know Joshua was now without power, as well as the rest of the inhabitants of the planet. With their advanced tracking equipment, they could lock onto any infrared heat signatures in the jungle within a certain radius from Joshua's last-known location.

The burn through the atmosphere was really turbulent, but when they broke through and were canvassed in a blue sky, the others in the pod all marveled aloud. It seemed like a lifetime ago that they had seen the sky. Sayid kept his focus on following the trajectory.

They came to a jungle and Sayid switched the monitor to view the infrared scan of the terrain below. The launched. Probably just as well, since the Council didn't allow any family besides their own, especially not one of their pawns' "handicapped" brothers.

Kent sighed and looked down the trail to his right. According to Marai, down this trail and over the river was the territory of a savage tribe. She believed her mother was being held in one of their villages, and was in danger of being killed. Marai had asked Kent to recon their villages and see if he could find her mother, then report back to them. Marai said they were pretty bloodthirsty and that he shouldn't attempt to rescue her mom unless she was in immediate danger. By her description of the tribe, it didn't sound like it was going to be easy.

They had given him one day to complete his mission. If he didn't return in one day, they would set off to rescue her themselves.

While he had been settling into his camp, Kent had clocked Hope's day from sunrise to sunrise, and knew their day was about one-and-five-eighths Earth hours shorter than he had grown up with. That gave him fewer than twenty-four hours to find a village—they didn't know how many miles away—scout the area, infiltrate the village, locate this woman whom he had never met, and report screen was immediately filled with red dots, indicating life-forms all over.

"Could those be the intelligent species?" Sayid asked Bo, who sat behind him. Bo leaned forward and looked at the screen.

"Maybe. It could also be animals in the rainforest. We will have to take a closer look."

"The *animals* could be intelligent, for all we know," Hannah added.

"Why didn't we just wait out the year for the EMP to diminish the population before risking coming down?" Groutage asked from the co-pilot's seat. Sayid shot him an angry look, widening his eyes a little and pursing his mouth.

"What EMP?" Hannah asked. "Did we launch an EMP on an intelligent species we haven't even began to try to make contact with?"

"Nukes, too," Bo added, looking out the side window.

Sayid turned around and looked at him: "How did you know?"

"You didn't think we would see the clouds of ash as we were coming down into the atmosphere? You are all the way his mind had been opened over the last few hours, any effort to persuade them was useless.

He had recognized Joshua's behavior when he came into their ship. It came from being raised in a home with an autistic brother. The agitated pacing, the busy hands, the word repeating; all very familiar to Kent. He used to be pretty close to his brother, keeping in touch with him on social media after he had enlisted. Nobody could make Kent laugh like Andrew: His observations were so clever! Kent would often post that he should go into standup comedy, even though he knew Andrew couldn't handle crowds very well. He thought maybe Andrew could learn to overcome his fear, just as he had with other social aspects. He had been smart enough to know his behavior didn't match others', and had worked very hard to fit in.

A wave of guilt swept over Kent as he stood there, alone. He had been so involved in his mercenary work after the military, that he had only visited Andrew in the States twice, each time one of their parents died. When the meteorite struck, Kent was too deeply involved in securing a seat on The Exodus for himself that he never even was able to speak to Andrew again before they really bad at keeping secrets."

"So we've declared *war* on them?!" Hannah asked, looking incredulous.

"Settle down!" Sayid shouted. He gained his composure before continuing. "You may as well know, since you were bound to find out sooner or later. When we came to the planet and concealed our ship behind the moon, we launched a drone toward the planet and they shot it out of the sky. So we weren't the ones to declare war. We just took the necessary measures to ensure our survival."

"Are you going to tell them about Joshua, too?" Groutage asked.

Sayid pulled his revolver out and fired a shot into Groutage's face, so the bullet would be stopped by the back of his helmet and not breach the ship. He slumped over, dead, and Hannah started screaming. Sayid holstered his weapon and went back to flying. He didn't need that *idiot* around, spilling Salman's secrets at every opportunity. He started to question why he even brought him in the first place, since he could probably locate Kent easily enough without Groutage's help.

He flew around for a while, looking for an open

a reward for bringing me back alive."

"It would be easier to haul a body back," Kent said. "Dead people don't kick you out of ships. And besides, how would I get you back to the Exodus? You know I can't fly."

"We both know Salman is not going to be content without knowing what happened to me. I wouldn't be surprised if he has already sent down a squad of mercenaries posing as a search party," Joshua said. "As far as I know, you could already be in contact with them."

"What is it going to take for you to trust me?" Kent asked.

"Find my mother," Marai said, without hesitation. "I think I know where she is."

Kent had a decision to make.

After being forced to sleep on the rough ground outside of the pod, he had awoken at first light and started down the trail leading back to his campsite. He now stood at the point where another trail branched off in a different direction. He had tried to convince them he wasn't going to harm them, but aside from them personally seeing into spot to land. Hannah was sobbing into the headset. Nobody dared say anything more to Sayid, which was how he preferred it.

Eventually, he spotted a clearing in the trees, big enough to land the pod on the jungle floor. He touched down and sat there for a moment before turning around and addressing Bo and Hannah.

"Here is where you go to work," Sayid said.

"What would you like us to do?" Bo asked.

"Make sure we can live as soon as we step out of the door."

Bo unlocked his seat from the floor, which allowed it to glide over to a side console and began running analyses on the oxygen content in the atmosphere. Hannah soon composed herself enough to join him. Sayid watched them both as they punched commands into the screens.

"The ship's readings say the air is breathable. It's very similar to the same atmospheric content of Earth," Bo said. "You should be able to exit the hatch without a breathing apparatus and be just fine."

"Well, then…?" Sayid said, as he strapped his respirator into place. Bo looked slowly over at Hannah,

"This is a part of what the sickness has done to him," Marai said.

"You don't catch autism like a cold, sweetheart," Kent said. "I know. I've seen it up close."

Joshua remembered reading about autism in his studies. Of course, the Council didn't allow anybody with any sort of perceived "defects" to ride along on their survival voyage, so Joshua had only learned about it from hearing or reading about it. His father talked about savants on Earth who were brilliant, but often had a form of autism called "Asperger's" as well. They displayed quirks similar to the ones he felt no control over now. Could it be possible that when his father had turned his genetic key for resistance to disease, he had also turned off the keys of social awkwardness? If that was possible, then a disease introduced into his normally powerful immune system for the first time might wreak havoc on the delicate balances put in place.

Maybe I _can_ catch autism, Joshua thought.

"How can we trust you?" Marai asked.

"Wouldn't you be dead already?" Kent asked, raising an eyebrow.

"Yes," Joshua agreed, "unless Salman also offered

who looked back at him.

"I'll go," she said, unbuckling and rising out of her seat. Li fastened on his respirator also, but Bo left his off, leading Sayid to believe either they were telling the truth, or they were suicidal. Hannah, pressed the lighted console next to the hatch and it slid open while a ramp extended. She took a few steps out, breathed in deeply a few times, then shot a look back at Sayid that said more than just a confirmation of her words.

"How long would it take a toxic atmosphere to kill someone un-acclimated to it?" Sayid asked Bo.

"Depending on the toxicity, it could be instant, it could be years," he replied. "But there are no toxins detected in the air—here, at least."

"What about the soil and water?" Sayid asked. "Are there any toxins we should know about?"

"I see now why it was so important that you bring us," Hannah said. "You only wanted us here to keep you alive."

"And I, in turn, will keep *you* alive," Sayid said. "I don't think you would like to be here alone without someone who knows how to use a gun and is willing to use it against a hostile species."

anymore!"

"What changed?" Joshua asked.

"Her," he said, pointing to Marai. "She was so sincere about saving your life, that I… I changed my mind. At first, when I heard you were sick, I thought I might just come along for the pleasure of watching you die. And I'll be honest, I *still* wanted you dead until about thirty minutes ago."

"What happened then?" Joshua asked.

"She took my hand and led me to you." Kent said, his eyes starting to moisten. "I can't explain it, but I could feel her concern for you and I started to pity you."

Joshua still looked at him with his head turned partway. He then cast a coy look at Marai, who was looking back at him. She had picked up the discarded knife and gripped it in her right hand like an icepick.

"What did you mean by 'autistic' just then?" Joshua asked, turning back to Kent. He wanted to de-escalate the tense situation.

"I didn't recognize it before, when I got the jump on you in this shuttle, but just a minute ago, I could tell. You hide your quirks pretty well, otherwise."

"I haven't always been like this," Joshua said.

"I know how to use a gun," Hannah said.

"Yes, but I wouldn't count on you having the guts to pull the trigger on a species you're more excited to study," Sayid said.

"Perhaps you're right," she said.

What did she mean by staring right at me while saying that?

"Study the soil," Sayid said, curtly. He walked around, noticing that he felt much lighter than he had on the ship. He realized the pull of gravity must not have been as strong as Earth's.

Hannah and Bo, meanwhile, had started gathering samples from the ground and nearby river and putting them in containers. Sayid watched them closely as she and Bo dipped strips into the liquid and inserted them into a slot on the tablets they held, reading the results onscreen. He saw Bo steal a glance at Hannah, making eye contact for a brief moment without exchanging any words. Then Bo immediately glanced over his shoulder at Sayid to see if he was still watching them.

"What are you finding?" Sayid asked Bo.

"Nothing," Hannah interjected. "It seems like this planet is habitable after all."

XI

"You need to go now," Marai said.

"I wasn't trying to hurt you!" Kent protested. "I was just trying to stop you from hurting me or yourself!"

"Then why did you come here with a knife?" Marai asked.

"It's *his* knife!" Kent said. "I was just returning it to him."

Joshua took one cautious step forward, watching Kent out of one eye. His hand scrawled a pattern down by his side. "I don't believe for a minute you were going to part with the one weapon I left you with out here." Marai gasped at hearing him talk.

"Okay, you know what? Fine!" Kent said angrily. "I was a little bit upset about the way you left me out here to die on a foreign planet, and maybe I spent a *little* bit of time plotting your death every time a strange growl kept me awake through the night! But I don't want to kill you

"Imagine our good fortune," Sayid said without any emotion in his voice. After an uneasy pause, Hannah immediately sprung into busying herself again.

"If it's okay, I would like to collect some plant samples for further study," she said.

"By all means…" Sayid said.

He returned to the interior and unbuckled Groutage, then heaved his lifeless body over his shoulder. He could hear blood dripping on the floor behind him, but he paid it no mind, since it would serve as a reminder of what insubordination reaped. He tossed the body callously out onto the jungle floor, and Hannah gasped a little.

"Don't bury him," Sayid warned. "I want to see what kinds of strange animals he will attract tonight. That should satisfy some of your scientific curiosity, eh?"

Hannah just nodded, with a wide-eyed look on her face. Sayid smiled.

That night, Sayid decided to send Li on a mission to examine the lifeforms they had picked up in their readings in order to see if he could locate the intelligent life responsible for building cities. This decision came about anyone!"

"No!" Joshua yelled. Marai struggled again, but his grip was too strong. Kent moved her right wrist into his hand holding her left and drew his knife from his belt.

"Marai!!" Joshua yelled, then he started hitting his own head with his stupid, useless fists.

Kent slid the knife across the floor to Joshua's feet, and released Marai, standing with his hands raised. "I don't want to kill Joshua!" he yelled. "I don't even want to take him back to the ship! He saved my life out here." He helped Marai to her feet and she ran over to Joshua, who was able to slow his pacing to a stop now.

Joshua was able to relax a bit when she stood next to him.

"I've had a lot to think about out here," Kent said, "and I'm pretty sure I was fighting for the wrong side when they refused to send anyone on a rescue mission. They don't care about me.

"I've got one question for you, though," Kent said. "Since when were you autistic?"

because Bo had noticed something interesting in the recordings of the infrared scans.

"There," he said. "When I pause it here you can see an anomaly that might suggest intelligent life. Most of the heat signatures are randomly placed, but these ones here are in a single-file line. That's not to say animals do not walk in straight lines, but given how little we have to go on, this might be a good place to start, sir."

"If it is an intelligent species, make sure you stay out of sight and return to me with some intel," Sayid ordered. "According to our flight path and their direction, they should only be about 10 kilometers to our west by now."

Li donned some night-vision goggles, adjusted some settings on his watch, then departed on a game trail with only a pistol holster draped over his black shirt. It only took a moment before he was swallowed up in the darkness of the trees.

"What do you want us to do?" Hannah asked Sayid.

"Watch the body, do something scientific; I don't care," Sayid said. "I am going into the pod to get some sleep. Wake me when Li returns."

"No, no, no, no, no," was all Joshua could verbalize. Kent took a few steps toward him, both hands raised, but Joshua could see the knife in his belt. Marai looked Joshua in his eyes as he screamed while pulling his hair. Something passed between them, but Joshua only hoped it was the right message.

Marai jumped into action, running toward Kent and trying to knock him out of the open doorway. He seemed ready for her and caught himself on the frame with both of his hands outstretched. His weight and muscle mass was too much for Marai's small frame to push any further, and he pulled himself back into the shuttle with ease. He fended off her blows, and caught both of her wrists as she tried to claw at his eyes.

Joshua tried to command his body to help, but all he could seem to do was pace back and forth, madly shaking his hands near his ears. He started to cry out in helpless frustration.

Marai tried kicking Kent in the groin, but he used his knees to block her, finally, sweeping her feet from underneath her and dropping her to the ground. He held onto her wrists as she fell, and he straddled her.

"Stop it!" Kent yelled. "I'm not going to hurt

It felt like Sayid had just fallen asleep when he was awoken by the report of two gunshots not too far off. He unlocked the pod hatch and hurried down the ramp to where Hannah and Bo stood huddled together, looking out into the dark jungle. Sayid strained his eyes to see into the blackness while pulling his coat up over his shoulders against the chill of the night.

"What is happening?" he demanded.

"There were gunshots," Bo said.

"I heard *that!* Could you see who fired them?"

"No, sir," Bo said. "But they came from over there." He pointed in the direction Li had departed from. They stood in silence for several minutes, listening to the night sounds of the jungle for any clues.

"I'm scared," Hannah said.

"Then get into the pod!" Sayid snapped. She ran up the ramp and started to close the hatch.

"Leave the door open," Sayid warned.

Soon, he could hear footsteps coming at a rapid pace. He brought his rifle to the ready position and flipped on the under-barrel flashlight. He watched patiently could prescribe. *Mmmmm, rat hair stew!*

As he paced around the room before sunset, he saw the rope ladder move and then pull tight. In the dim light, he could see two figures ascending the ladder, but he couldn't make out the features of either one. He stepped back and continued pacing along the far bulkhead. Soon, he saw Marai's face lit up from the dim sunset light coming in from the side window. She looked… tired?

After she pulled herself up into the pod, she came over and gave Joshua a hug. He was excited to show her how he had learned to speak. He brought his hand up near his head to start writing in the air, when he looked over and saw her companion pulling himself up into the pod.

Kent Waller, the man who had tried to ambush Joshua as he made his escape, was now standing in the very doorway out of which Joshua had pushed him. Immediately, Joshua's hands started flying around near his head, uncontrollably. He *had* to tell Marai, but he couldn't control his body enough to make the physical connection to his verbal ability. He started pacing, covering his head and pointing at Kent over, and over again.

"What is it, Joshua?" Marai asked, panic in her voice.

through the scope for any movement in the jungle. He heard Li before he saw him.

"It's me!" he yelled, possibly preventing his untimely demise. Sayid removed his finger from the trigger, but continued to watch through the scope. Li came running into view, clutching his shoulder with one hand while his arm dangled helplessly to his side.

When he came into the light, Sayid lowered his rifle and asked him what had happened.

"It's people! Humans!"

"Humans?" Bo asked.

"Yes! They look like us, except more primitive."

"Did they shoot you?" Sayid asked.

"The gunshots were mine," Li said, starting to catch his breath. "I was walking along the path when I heard movement, so I hid off in the bushes about twenty meters. I couldn't believe it when I saw a tribe of hunters who were human walking down the path."

"How do you know they were hunters?" Sayid asked.

"Two of them were carrying something in a net that they had captured. I couldn't make out what it was, because as they started coming closer, one of them left the

WOOD/LIFEBLOOD

Joshua couldn't help but be nervous when Marai was away for long. She seemed pretty sure of herself, but she had told him how she was not from the jungle, and he wondered how she managed to stay safe with all the dangers out there. There must have been predators out there, maybe some even more dangerous than the ones on Earth he had read about. She had mentioned a "puma," and he wondered if this was the same large feline or something else, entirely. In his few days of study upon landing on the planet, he had noticed some of the smaller animals he observed were very similar to Earth creatures, almost as if they were following a universal evolutionary blueprint. There were some significant adaptive changes, as well as some size and color differences, but given the limited variety of species that had been categorized on Earth, these could very well be within the realm of...

Joshua realized he was letting his mind wander in order to quell his fear for Marai's safety. It was starting to get dark, and she still hadn't come back.

Who was she going to bring back to help him? Was there some medicine man in a nearby village? Joshua shuddered at the thought of all the strange procedures a witch doctor could perform, as well as the medicines he path and started walking straight toward me! His face was painted white, like a skull, but he apparently could see in the darkness.

"I thought maybe it was just chance that he was walking in my direction, and that if I held still he would walk past me. Then he nocked an arrow and shot me in the shoulder!" Li removed his hand to show the stump of a broken arrow protruding from a blood-soaked shirt. "I shot him twice and started to run here, but I don't know if I killed him!"

"Those shots sounded pretty close," Sayid said, now turning his attention back to the jungle. "They might have followed you." He unslung his rifle once again and started scanning the jungle paths surrounding them.

Bo excused himself to the pod. Li hastily wrapped his shoulder, donned his night-vision goggles once again, and held his pistol at his side.

Once again, the jungle noises filled their ears as they scanned in silence.

"Don't you think we should leave, sir?" Li asked.

"I want to get a look," Sayid said. As he scanned the jungle, he thought he saw a skull on the ground and took a closer look. He realized too late that it was a man

"I have an idea," she said. "All I need you to do is empty your mind. You seem like you'd be pretty expert at that."

"Are you clowning me right now?" he asked.

"Just stop talking and stop thinking."

"Yes, ma'am," he said, glaring at her.

"And close your eyes," she added. He rolled his eyes, but finally gave in and shut his eyes. She grabbed onto his hand. *Maybe I can do this for both of us?*

Marai emptied her mind and started moving in the direction of the pod. He stumbled around at first and she had to shush him when he cursed, but after a few dozen steps, she could feel the light start to uphold them. Her pace stayed the same, but the pace of time around her slowed. Their footsteps became surer, and pretty soon, they neared the waterfall canyon. Marai slowed her pace and looked back at Kent. He wore a wide grin across his face.

"I feel *really* good!" he said. "Can all of you extra-terrestrials do this?"

"Not that I know of," she said. "And I believe *you're* the extra-terrestrial."

with a skull painted on his face, and the man stood and stabbed himself in the heart, falling to the ground with the grin still spread across his face.

"Did you see that?" Sayid asked Li in a hushed voice.

"Yes, sir." Li responded. "Why did he kill himself?"

"I don't know. But keep watching for any others."

Sayid thought he could hear the faint sound of leaves moving in the jungle, but he wasn't sure if he was imagining it, or if more of these suicidal hunters were out there.

"I think it's time to go," he told Li.

Sayid and Li carefully started backing toward the pod with their guns at the ready. Just as Sayid was about to sling his rifle, he felt something reach out and grab his ankle. He looked down and saw the corpse of Donny Groutage gripping him tightly, while his head still fell loosely backward, mouth agape and eyes closed.

"What the...?!" he shouted. Hannah screamed from the interior of the pod. Sayid's heart was so filled with fear that he dropped his rifle to the ground. In his panic, all he could think of doing was trying to escape the

"Look, I don't know what happened. All I know is I was here in the jungle with my mom, staying with a tribe that doesn't exactly have access to the news, then they were all killed by a murderous tribe, after which I met Joshua and he got really sick, and my mom is missing, and I need to go find her because I fear the murderous tribe has taken her captive. So instead of standing out here debating the past, can we figure out a way to move into the future?"

"Well, sogg-e-e," Kent said as he stood up and brushed off his backside.

"You are so odd," Marai said.

Marai tried to teach Kent how to light-walk. At first he refused to remove his boots, but after she showed him again how she could "disappear," he decided he would give it a try. He complained about how uncomfortable the ground was, cursed her chicken feet, and made a show of walking over smooth dirt like it was hot coals. He wasn't getting it, and the day was growing late. Marai wanted to be out of the jungle in case any predators—or worse—happened by on a night hunt.

She would have to figure something else out.

clutches of this dead man. The more he moved, the tighter Grouch gripped. His other hand reached up and grabbed Sayid's calf, as he started to climb upward.

In a desperate effort to survive, Sayid pulled out his pistol and fired all six shots point-blank into Grouch's face. Grouch kept climbing, despite being six rounds deader. Sayid tried to push him off, but as he did so, Grouch caught hold of his wrist. A garbled sound came from his throat as he tried to pull what was left of his face up near Sayid's. The noise morphed into something that sounded like words.

"Kil-l-l-l him-m-m-m," Sayid heard.

He was frightened in earnest now, and started whimpering as he stood frozen. A machete sliced through the air, taking the corpse's arms off at the elbows. Sayid found himself freed from the terrible grasp, and ran into the ship without noticing at the time that it was Li who had come to his rescue. He punched the console controls to raise the ramp and close the door after Li was inside.

As the door slid closed, a frantic, high-pitched voice rang out in the jungle:

"Help me!"

attention to the passage of time, is all."

"But, that was like Speedy Gonzales type of fast!"

Marai looked at him and furrowed her brows. "Speedy Who?"

"You know, the cartoon mouse that says, Yi-pa and then zips off in a cloud?"

"Oh, that must be an Earth thing," Marai said. "The planet, not the god."

"Wait, you're saying…" Kent said.

"I'm not from Earth, Kent. I'm from here."

Kent plopped down onto the trail, removed his hat, and rubbed his forehead. "Wait… so… how are you speaking English?"

"I wondered the same thing about Joshua when I first met him. What are the chances alien invaders speak our same language?"

"Invaders? What did Joshua tell you?"

"He told me he had escaped from your ship and that you had plans to wipe out our people without being provoked."

"Without being… did he tell you about how y'all shot down our drone before we could contact you? You call that *not* being provoked?"

9

Hugh groaned as he knelt down next to the river. His shoulder throbbed where he had removed a bullet not too long ago, and his knees protested against the hard ground as he brought the water up and scrubbed the grime off his face. How did he ever allow himself to get so old?

Just the little exertion it took in doing this simple task took its toll on his stamina. He placed his hands on the ground, shut his eyes tightly, and breathed through pursed lips as the water dripped off his face.

"It's not enough," Jack said.

Hugh looked into the water and saw Jack's reflection as he stood behind him.

"You need to live up to your calling," Jack said.

"It's a little hard to judge people when they don't require justice," Hugh replied.

"Oh, there's plenty of people out there behaving wickedly."

Marai was completely surprised to find him standing upright, almost in the exact same place she had left him. She slowed her running pace and came out of her trance in front of him.

"What *in the name of all that is holy* is going on here?!" he exclaimed.

"I'm beating you in a race," Marai said.

"You just disappeared!" Kent said. "And then reappeared over there!"

"What are you talking about?" Marai said. "I just started running—like I told you I could—and you stood here like an idiot."

"No, I know what I saw!" Kent was gesturing excitedly as he spoke. "Y'all up and disappeared, vanished, poof! I stood up to see if I was seeing things, and then you reappear right before my eyes in a different spot!"

"I didn't do anything except clear my mind and run. If it seemed like I had disappeared, maybe I was running faster than I thought I was?"

"That's pretty fast if you can zip out of sight in an instant," Kent said.

"I don't know… it doesn't seem like I'm traveling down the trail any faster, I'm just not paying as much

"Yeah, but I suspect many of them have been wiped out with the bombs."

"Along with many innocent people," Jack said.

"Yes, I imagine so," Hugh said. "But I feel like things are getting out of balance. Even the innocent who were left behind are starting to do desperate things in order to survive. Chaos is pushing us to lose our humanity."

"You're not talking about yourself, are you, Hugh?"

"No. At least I hope not."

"You can't be an unrighteous judge. It doesn't work that way," Jack said. "You would lose it all."

"The world has never been this bad. Even before the attack, we were nearing the brink of global war for the first time in our history. Not only that, but we've probably lost all of our records. People will forget their past. Our language will be lost. Even more misunderstandings, and fighting, and… and…"

"Destruction?" Jack asked.

"Yes."

"So what is your plan in all of this?" Jack asked.

"I'm still going down to the mountain," Hugh

"That doesn't make any sense," Kent confirmed.

"I can't explain it, but when I clear my mind and get rid of some physical burdens, I can travel a lot faster."

"You consider *shoes* a burden?" he asked. "It seems like you could use such a burden right now."

She stopped and let out an exasperated sigh, then turned to face him. "Look, I'll show you," she said. "Try to keep up with me."

"Hold on," Kent said, lowering into a starting-block stance. "You're going to have to give me a head start first." Marai rolled her eyes.

"Are you going to say go, or should…"

Marai emptied her mind and took off. She glanced back to see if he was close behind, and was surprised to see he wasn't even visible on the trail behind her. Did he somehow get ahead of her? She ran a bit more and was confused when she didn't see him on a straight stretch on the trail ahead. *Maybe he fell down?*

The words in her mind brought her out of her trance-like state, and she determined in a few moments to go back and make sure he was okay. She turned around and emptied her mind once again, running in the direction she had just come from.

said. "Even if I'm no longer on an official mission, and the government for which I work is most likely gone, I still feel like I need to make contact with the visitors."

"Why do you feel that way?"

"Call it a hunch." Hugh said. "I'm wondering if maybe they weren't trying to make contact with us and we blew it."

"Literally," Jack said.

Hugh chuckled. The break in mood was almost like a cue for him to get up and get moving. He grunted and lifted his aching bones up from the ground. As he turned to walk back to his car, he heard Jack call out his name. He looked back into the reflective surface of the water.

"Be careful," Jack said. "I don't have the same hunch."

In his absence, a mob had surrounded his car and were going through his belongings. One man held the reins to his horses, who had been unhitched from the frame.

X

Marai understood now how frustrating it must have been for Xrys to wait for her every few steps going up the Sacred Mountain. She really wanted to light-walk, like she had done in order to get here, but if she did, she would end up just leaving Kent far behind. To make matters worse, she had left her shoes back with Joshua, and when she wasn't light-walking, her feet ceased to be conduits of healing, opting instead for the opposite.

So she moved forward, carefully watching where she set each foot while leading the way. At this rate, they would get back in a few days, and probably find Joshua had started stabbing the bedding with IV needles.

"Don't you have some shoes or something?" Kent asked from behind her.

"I don't normally use them when I have to travel fast," Marai answered. As soon as she said it, she knew it probably didn't make any sense.

"What are you doing?" Hugh announced. They all turned and looked at him, but they didn't seem particularly surprised.

"We're taking these things for the King of New London," a man said as he approached Hugh, holding Hugh's rifle in his hands. Hugh quickly assessed his situation and counted thirty-four men, all armed in some way. Way too many for him to judge by himself, or even with Tai's and Borghaus' help. He felt a knot in his back start to tighten.

"And who would that be?" Hugh asked. "I wasn't aware of any monarchs on Hope."

"You're looking at him," the man said. "King Donovan the First."

"Hail to the King!" a man yelled from the crowd to a few chuckles.

"You're aware New London is a pile of ashes now?" Hugh asked.

"Out of the ashes arose a new king," Donovan said. "And I'm looking to expand our borders beyond the city. Can I count on your loyalty, or do you need to be gunned down where you stand?"

At these words, the men all pointed their weapons

"You need *my* help?"

"I can't leave him alone," Marai said, "I need to go find my mother. I think she's in trouble."

He dumped the water he was boiling over the fire to extinguished it partially. "I'll go with you," he said. "But you're going to have to explain some things on the way."

"Fine," she said.

He climbed a tree and went into his makeshift hut, emerging from the opening with a pack.

"You won't need that," she said. "I plan on traveling fast, and we have sleeping gear and food back with Joshua."

He tossed his pack back into the hut.

"Whatever," he said. He climbed back down and started walking with her down the trail she came from.

"I guess you should know my name if we're going to be traveling together," he said.

"My name is Sergeant Kent Waller."

at Hugh. Hugh looked around to see if he could see Tai and Borghaus anywhere. He gave a light tug on their tethers and they appeared, standing behind the mob. Tai looked hungry.

"I'm afraid you won't be taking anything that belongs to me today," Hugh said.

The men oohed at his defiance.

"And who are you that stares at death so boldly?" Donovan asked?

Hugh chucked at the irony. "Hugh Winters," he said.

"President Wyndham's Chief Judge?" Donovan said. "I heard stories about you!"

"You'd be better off believing them," Hugh said. He released thirty-two more captives to each stand behind a man.

"Now there's the problem," Donovan said. "I've sworn to take down Capital, and you just happen to be one of the first men on my hit list. I'd say there's a pretty good chance you're not leaving here alive, even if you *were* to pledge allegiance to me."

"If you can enter in, they have murderous intentions," Hugh said.

song which had existed in many forms to him—including visual—that had given him back his words?

He dropped the pen and made writing motions in the air.

"I love you, Marai," he said to no one.

Marai moved through the jungle at a blinding speed, unhindered by the shoes she had left at the base of the ladder. She drew light and strength from the planet up through her bare feet, and let go of her thoughts as she hurried toward her destination. The jungle almost looked frozen in time around her, as if she was moving through time at a different rate.

She didn't trouble herself with directions, she just let Mother Hope guide her. She had a mental image in her head of where she needed to go, and that was enough. Within a few hours she reached her destination.

The man startled and looked up from his campfire.

"It's you again!" he said.

"My name is Marai," she said. "I need your help. I have Joshua Hawker with me and he is in bad shape."

"What is *that* supposed to mean?" Donovan said, looking confused.

"But wait for my command," Hugh said. Tai, Borghaus, and the others all took a step forward. Many disappeared from Hugh's sight, but some remained.

"Who are you talking to?" Donovan demanded, looking around nervously. When he didn't see anyone around, he steeled his resolve and raised his rifle to his shoulder.

"My legion," Hugh said to Donovan, looking him straight in the eyes.

"Kill him!" Donovan yelled.

"Now!" Hugh shouted.

All but six men fell down dead. The six survivors looked at their dead leader and friends and dropped their rifles, running off into the trees.

Hugh took a few steps forward and addressed Donovan, who now stood bare before him.

"What happened to me?" Donovan yelled, shaking and staring at his hands.

Before him on the ground lie his dead body. Behind Donovan, twenty-eight men were also trying to come to terms with their untimely demise.

didn't know where to go from here. Should he hop on one foot or pat his head and have a list that Marai would understand as interpretations of his nonverbal cues? That gave him another idea: Maybe he could just learn sign language along with her? But how would they do that, unless she already knew some form of sign language and could teach it to him? All of his reference material on the servers was destroyed when the EMP was launched.

There was something with his idea about *the list* though. Something he could use…

His hands shook even more as his fingers flew into a tizzy. *What was it he was trying to get at?*

Writing.

He hadn't yet tried communicating in one of the most basic ways. He fumbled with the latch on a cabinet, but finally opened it and pulled out a piece of paper and a pen. He clicked the pen and began writing the first thing that came into his mind.

"Lacrimosa dies illa, Qua resurget ex favilla, Judicandus homo reus," he said aloud. It was the lyrics to Lacrimosa from Mozart's requiem. Joshua started laughing. He was able to speak the words he was writing! His motor skills were guiding his verbal abilities! But was it *just* this

"You gave up your right to life when you took up arms and decided to take mine," Hugh told Donovan. "All of you did!" he told the rest.

"The remainder of the life you would have lived will now add to my lifespan."

"Meanwhile, you will live a life of captivity inside of me, unable to act independently, unable to speak, unable to satisfy your addictions, only eating when I eat, and only able to be free when I allow you to."

"You better explain 'free' to them, boss," Tai said. As if in response to his request, one of the mob tried to run away before Hugh could "capture" him. The fugitive suddenly realized he had been caught with a golden tether woven into his soul when he was yanked off his feet. Hugh quickly reeled the man into himself. The man's screaming ceased when he was swallowed up inside of Hugh's body. Hugh noticed the pains of aging had gone, and he felt like he was in the prime of his life once again. He must have been young and in good shape. The others all looked down and saw a similar tether attached to them.

Donovan looked around and noticed many others standing around who weren't among his men.

"There are more with me than there were with

WOOD/LIFEBLOOD

Joshua remembered reading somewhere that about fifty-five percent of communication was nonverbal. Cues people gave with their hands, stance, expressions on their faces, etc. Just the slightest flexing of one muscle in the face could create a totally different expression, and human beings were especially attuned to those cues. Thirty-seven percent of communication was tone-of-voice, and while it was possible she heard the desperation in his one word, "I," she probably got more from his body language than from that one word. That only left eight percent of communication which were the actual words spoken.

I don't need words as much as I think I do.

Joshua noticed that he had stopped pacing and was now standing in front of a mirror. He smiled, but his eyes stayed the same when he did. He used to smile with his whole face; eyes squinting, nose wrinkling. He tried to frown, but noticed how unconvincing it was that he was angry, even to himself. He couldn't make any expressions that people would understand at a deeper level of communication!

He shook his hands violently up by his head, trying to put this together. He knew he was close, but he you," Hugh said. "They only have power to enter in and take a life when a person weakens themselves to the point of no return. But I remain the Chief Judge, and the moment you take up arms with the intent to kill, I pass judgment."

"I'm sorry you didn't believe the stories," Hugh said.

"Wait, no…!" Donovan shouted.

He pulled them all inside of himself with the exception of Tai and Borghaus.

"Maybe I get a deputy badge now, boss?" Tai asked.

"Shut up," said Borghaus.

back and forth as he thought through his current situation.

When he robbed the social center of his prefrontal cortex in order to re-train it to operate motor skills, he must have short-circuited some of his other functions. Maybe reassigning this specific area of his brain to handle motor skills had had an effect on his compulsory drive. Regardless, there was no amount of logic that could seem to stop him from doing it. He *knew* he was pacing, he *knew* it was odd, but here he was doing it anyway.

His biggest concern at the moment was his inability to form a complete verbal sentence. He could think in sentences—speaking was easy in his brain—but he couldn't get his vocal cords to follow suit. He paced back and forth for hours, trying to figure out how to speak. Every time he tried, he would stutter and fail, then anxiety would set in and he would have to pinch his fingers together up near his ears, as if trying to get his brain to do what he asked.

Marai knew what I was trying to say, even though I barely spoke this morning. Why was that? What was I doing that made us communicate?

Doing.

That's it! I was pointing to myself when I tried to speak.

10

"Why did you leave that person there?!" Hannah demanded.

"I don't know if you noticed the dead body of Grouch trying to kill me or not," Sayid said, as he landed the ship on the rock outcropping.

"Someone was out there calling for help! Someone from the ship, calling out in English! It could be this 'Joshua' you're trying to find!"

Sayid turned off the engines and lit the interior so he could look into her face. "I don't care," he said, bluntly. "I might as well tell you, since you were bound to find out anyway."

"Tell me what?" Hannah asked.

"We're not here to rescue Joshua." There was silence as the implications of that statement sunk in.

"Who is this Joshua, anyway?" Bo asked.

Sayid didn't think he needed to tell them *everything*. "He's an enemy of the Council. He went rogue

Joshua had never been kissed by a girl before. Strangely enough, this felt more like the protective kisses his dad used to plant on his head when he was younger, rather than a romantic kiss. Regardless, he appreciated it. Marai was truly concerned about his welfare, even though he was working through recovery at a rapid pace.

Work on his motor skills, she said. He might as well see how he was progressing since the reassignment of his prefrontal cortex. He set his feet upon the ground and stood with just a little instability. He took a few steps forward, and was amazed that his body was responding to his will, however weakly. This was something that took most people months or even years of physical therapy. His hands were a little surer in their movement, although he wouldn't trust himself to give anyone a haircut just yet. What he didn't understand were his urges. It made no sense to him that his body felt like it needed to rock back and forth when he felt anxiety. The urge was beyond his ability to control. He also would hold up his hands near his head, trying to do *something,* but it was like his body didn't know what. Even now, he was doing something he didn't understand, nor think he could control: He was pacing and is trying to turn the population of this planet against us. He escaped on a ship to the planet's surface with an SF agent, Kent Waller, who was supposed to stop him. We still have no idea if Kent succeeded or not."

"Hence, your arrival," Hannah said.

"Yes."

"That voice sounded either female or young," Bo said. "Is Joshua young?"

"He's old enough to know what he's doing. Or *un*doing," Sayid said.

"And you're just going to leave him out there to fend for himself?" Hannah asked.

"Like I said, this is not a rescue mission," Sayid said. "Not in Joshua's case, anyway."

"So what do we do now?" Hannah said.

"We lock the hatches and sleep. I'll make a decision in the morning."

Bo didn't even know anyone else was awake until he felt the ship move. Sayid sat at the controls, silhouetted by the rising sun. Li sat next to him in the copilot's seat. Bo decided to stay in his bunk and try to decide what was

"They only will if they can find him. I know what I must do." Marai opened her eyes and stood.

She felt enough strength to do something for Joshua she should have thought of days ago. He was helpless in his current state, and wouldn't be able to keep up with Marai if she was going to go for help, so she would have to bring help to him. She looked over and saw he was already awake, but still lying down.

"I'm going to go get help," she told him. "You need someone here with you while I go save my mother."

He struggled to sit up, then pointed at himself.

"I…" he said.

"You want to go, yes," she said. "I would take you, but I'm going to be travelling very fast. I'm only going about a half-day's journey downriver. I should be back tonight."

"Marai," he said. He started rocking back and forth, trying to speak.

"I'll be okay," she said. "You can work on your motor skills while I'm gone." She rubbed her hand where he had tried to inject the needle and laughed.

She stood up, hesitated, and then bent and kissed him on the forehead before descending the rope ladder.

going on from there.

Sayid flew low over the trees, scanning the ground as he went. Bo guessed they were looking for signs of the SF agent or the pod he had flown in. After a few hours, when the sun was higher in the sky, Li pointed to something off to his right.

"What do you think they have found?" Hannah asked from the bunk adjacent to his.

"I'm not sure," he replied. The ship started to circle and descend.

"I think we're about to find out," Hannah said.

Bo decided it was time to let her in on his plan. "I want to go find the boy," Bo whispered. "That cry for help sounded so desperate."

"Sayid won't let you," Hannah whispered back. "You've seen what he does to people who go against him!"

"I have a plan," Bo said. He pulled a water-filtering straw out of the bag stowed underneath his bed. He flipped open a small pocketknife and started digging out the insides of the straw, keeping a wary eye on Li and Sayid as he did. He dumped out the ceramic dust and replaced it with foam cut out of his mattress pad.

"Sayid is going to get really sick," Bo said.

IX

The enemy has seen you, Marai. They know you have found He-Who-Saves.

Marai heard Xrys' voice in her head as she meditated. She had spent the day recovering from her spirit walk, and was surprised to discover she could hear Xrys while in the body.

The Dark Priest used my physical eyes to see through my spiritual eyes as I stood guard.

"How do you know he did?" Marai asked.

Because I saw through my physical eyes too, when they were awakened into use.

"So they know where we are?" she asked.

I do not know. I need to tell you something else: They have your mother. She is in a village along a cliff wall.

"I need to go find her!" Marai said.

You must not leave him alone. In his weakened state, they will kill him.

"Bo, you can't leave me here with this lunatic!" Hannah said.

"I don't intend to," Bo said. "We're going to find our life here."

Hannah nodded and then slipped quietly out of her bunk, keeping an eye on Sayid.

"What are you doing?" Bo whispered. He furiously gestured for her to come back.

Hannah looked back and mouthed, "Plan B." He watched as she reached into a drawer, pulled something small out, and set it under Sayid's pillow. She snuck back and told Bo, "Stay away from Sayid's bed."

Hannah felt the ship rock slightly, indicating they had landed. She watched closely as Sayid unbuckled and armed himself, making sure to reload his pistol. He dropped the box of bullets into a drawer and went to the door.

"You're coming with us," Sayid told her and Bo. They got up and put on their boots.

"Where are we going?" Hannah asked, as she gathered gear into her pack.

"What we believe is real," Ka'ar said. "Let me show you,"

Kit started to try to escape the clutches of her captor, fearing she was about to be harmed or killed. His grip tightened around her arms. She saw another soul eater approach the macabre chief holding a pouch. He reached in and pulled out a pair of bloodied eyeballs.

"I have sacrificed my body so that I could have great spiritual power," he said. "Now I will look through the Traitor's eyes and find her."

"Xrys!" Kit whispered.

He put the eyeballs into his empty sockets and started to stare past everyone. The drum and eerie singing started again. He stood there for a while, then made an announcement:

"She is with the Wretched Boy!" A cheer went up.

"The only thing powerful enough to stop creation is its destruction!" Ka'ar yelled.

They chanted again: "Destroy."

He removed the eyeballs and placed them back in the bag. Then he turned his hollow gaze back upon Kit.

"And as for you, woman;" he said, gesturing to an empty cage suspended above them, "you will be the bait!"

"Li spotted a parachute stretched out in a tree a few hundred yards downriver from here. Now move."

"Can we at least have guns?" Hannah asked.

"No, you can't," Sayid said, bluntly.

"We will protect you," Li said. She noticed that he now carried a machete across his back in addition to his rifle. Both of them were dressed in camouflage.

Sayid opened the hatch and lowered the ramp. They led the way out of the pod, both of them surveying the area with guns drawn. When they saw the area was clear, Sayid looked back at Hannah and Bo and nodded for them to follow.

They didn't speak as they traveled along the riverbank. Hannah could tell Sayid was much warier of this strange planet than he was the night before. Occasionally, one of them would hold up a fist, which Hannah understood to mean stop, since they did so themselves. They would look around, sometimes turning an ear to the jungle or squatting and looking at tracks. Satisfied that they were safe, Sayid would beckon them on.

They eventually reached the parachute in the trees and saw that someone had made a permanent camp in the area. The ground had a few rows of cultivated plants, some

He was terrible to look upon! His skin was burned and stretched in thin webs all over his body, spikes pierced his sinewy muscles, and his lips, nose, and eyes were missing entirely. His head truly *did* resemble a skull, not just one painted on. As he stopped in front of Kit, he tilted his head down and the hollow black holes in his head seemed to bore through her. She tried to turn away, but the soul eater behind her grabbed her face and forced her to look at him.

"What do you want with my daughter!" Kit said through gritted teeth.

He opened his mouth and a rumbling voice came out of his throat, even though his mouth didn't form any words: "It is the Destroyer who wants her. We will do his work and consume all."

"Why does she need to be destroyed?" Kit said as she struggled to free her face from the soul eater's grip. "What does my daughter have to do with any of this?"

"She is the Seer of our enemy. She and the Wretched Boy must be destroyed."

"Destroy," the tribe chanted in unison behind Kit.

"I can't believe you think my daughter is involved in any of your… superstitions!" she spat.

of which looked like peas with new blossoms on them. There was a rock ring for a fire, and up in the trees, underneath the parachute, a hut-like shelter had been built. Sayid kept his gun in his hands and called out.

"Kent? Kent, are you here?"

There was no answer.

"Waller?" Li yelled, a little louder. After no answer, he slung his rifle and climbed up the tree to look inside the hut. He emerged to announce, "He's not here, but this is definitely his camp." He held up a Special Forces pack to show everyone.

"Where could he be?" Sayid asked, mostly to himself. He knelt down and hovered his hand over the black coals of the fire. "It's still warm," he said to Li.

"Do you think he's been captured or killed?" Li asked.

"No signs of a struggle in the footprints around here," Sayid said as he surveyed the ground. "Although…"

"What is it?" Li asked, coming over after having descending the tree.

"Look at these sets of footprints in the dust. They are pretty fresh, since the shape of the steps haven't been upset by any wind or rain. They're side-by-side, and one is made Kit lose hope in surviving.

She reached up to rub a sore spot on her head only to discover dried blood had matted her hair. They must have hit her pretty brutally when they knocked her unconscious. Her temples pulsed with a dull throbbing.

As they neared the center of the village, a screaming mob of dirty women and children started to throw rocks at her. She ducked her head between her knees, but could only protect so much with her hands tied behind her back.

The men porting her stopped moving, and the screaming died down. She was dropped unceremoniously on the ground, and the net holding her was cut open. A soul eater grabbed her by the arm and lifted her to her feet in front of an altar. She could guess what they had planned for her.

"Ka'ar, we have brought the mother of Marai!" he yelled into the cave opening before them.

The men started to hum in deep, dissonant tones, and a drum started to beat a steady, throbbing rhythm which vibrated inside of Kit's chest. The cacophonic singing swelled into a crescendo as a dark figure emerged from the bowels of the cave.

barefoot. They're definitely smaller than an adult's feet."

"Could the boy be with him?"

"Possibly," Sayid said.

Hannah wanted to know if the voice they heard could belong to the smaller set of footprints: "Do they go in the same direction we came from?"

"Negative," Li said. "We heard the voice about twenty miles in *that* direction. These prints are too fresh to have been made by the same person. Unless this was the starting point for a marathon."

"Then who out there knew how to say 'help me' in English?" Hannah asked.

"Maybe these prints belong to someone else?" Li mused. "Perhaps Waller is making friends with the natives."

"That would seem more likely," Sayid said. "I think Joshua would be wearing boots; this extra set of prints are bare."

"I'm still trying to wrap my mind around the idea that the inhabitants of this place look human," Bo said. "What are the chances? Unless that's the universal model…"

"Later!" Sayid snapped. Then to Li he said, "I

through the air, and she started to fear her window of opportunity was closing. She had to let them know she was here, held captive by these awful men!

"Help me!" she screamed as loudly as she could.

She didn't remember being knocked unconscious.

The impaled skulls atop pikes were the first thing that let Kit know they were nearing a Lamek village. They passed through a heavy gate made from tree trunks, which was swung shut behind them. The village was surrounded by a wall made of similarly-sharpened poles. It formed a semi-circle until it ran into a rocky cliff wall which stretched upward at a very steep angle. There were caves cut into the cliff wall, which looked like dwellings connected by ladders and walkways. There were also huts scattered about, some raised up on heavy stilts. Nothing grew on the ground inside of the village wall, it was all dirt and stone.

As they passed under a walkway, Kit looked up and saw a hanging cage made with jagged spikes, swaying ominously back and forth. The skeletal remains of some soul unfortunate enough to be captured by the Lamek rotted inside of the cage. All the signs of death around her suggest we bring some gear from the ship and stay here for a while. Maybe he will return."

"Hannah and I will go back to the ship and bring back the gear," Bo said.

"Hannah will stay here with me, while *you and Li* go get the gear," Sayid corrected.

"Whatever you say, sir," Bo said. "But first, I need a drink." He pulled the filter straw from his pack and bent over the clear water of the river with his back to Sayid. Hannah could see he didn't really use the straw, but just pretended to. He stood up, wiping his mouth.

"Anybody else thirsty?" Hannah watched as Sayid eyed Bo while checking his canteen. It was empty.

"You can use my filter, sir," Bo offered. "It's completely safe."

Sayid took the straw and walked over to the water. He squatted down and stayed there for a long moment.

"Hannah," Sayid said without turning. "Come show me how to use this."

Bo said, "It's just like a straw. You just…"

"*Show* me," Sayid demanded.

Hannah had seen the biological readings with Bo. She knew that they were not compatible with the biology trees, and one of them plunged a spear into the ground underneath her, point up, to discourage her from trying to shake herself free. Then he notched an arrow and started creeping forward slowly, while his companion stayed at Kit's side. Besides her lone guard, the entire party all crept toward the light area, staying in the shadows as much as possible.

"Watch closely," her guard said. "You are about to see a blood sacrifice."

She watched as a figure stood, silhouetted by the light, and stabbed himself in the chest, collapsing immediately.

"He sacrifices his body to take another," the sentry said.

The warriors started creeping forward again. Kit thought she could hear muffled voices, which suddenly went quiet.

Then very clearly, she heard someone shout in English, "What the…?!" followed by a piercing scream and six gunshots. There was a scuffle of some sort, but she was too far away to see who was involved or what was happening. Whatever was taking place sounded horrific, with guttural noises and growling. Something whipped of this planet, and until they adapted and built up immunity—which may even take a generation or two—consuming unfiltered water could be very dangerous, even deadly. Sayid still looked at her intensely, holding out the straw in his hand.

"I will show you," Bo said, stepping forward before Hannah could decide what to do. He took the straw from Sayid's hand and bent over the flowing water. He drew in a sip of water.

"Just like that," Bo said.

"More," Sayid said.

"But I've already drank enough…"

"MORE!" Sayid shouted, now drawing his pistol and pointing it at Bo's temple. Bo nodded silently, then bent over to drink more water from the river.

"Keep drinking," Sayid said. "Until I say."

"What is this all about?" Hannah asked, trying not to sound frightened.

"I just want to make sure Bo is hydrated for his journey," Sayid said. Bo tried to pull the straw out of the water and Sayid pushed his head down.

"KEEP DRINKING!" he yelled into Bo's ear. Another thirty seconds must have passed in frightened heard some noise behind her in the bushes. A quick glance back revealed a vacated spot in the trail where the soul eater once was. She strained her eyes to see if she could determine his whereabouts, and then saw movement off to her left. He had left the trail and was making his way to some unknown destination in the dark jungle. Almost as soon as he was out of sight, two loud reports sounded from the jungle, accompanied by muzzle flashes. *Someone had a gun!*

The Lamek all left the trail and started walking quietly through the undergrowth. Her captors carried her with them, rather than leave her by the trail unattended. Kit was hoping they were heading into a fight where she might have a chance to escape or be rescued. The fact that they didn't hear any more gunshots made her wary of making any sudden attempts. She would bide her time until she could see what the situation was.

Beams of light became visible through the trees. She started to hope someone with advanced weapons was out there. She could see an area in the trees that was lit up, but the men carrying her stopped before she could see what was creating the light. They hung the pole from which her net was suspended from the branches of two silence. Hannah didn't know what to do.

"That's enough."

Bo sat up coughing and gasping. Sayid grabbed his arm and pulled him roughly to his feet. "Bring me back a sealed bottle of water from the pod," Sayid hissed, then he shoved him off in the direction of the pod. Li walked behind him as they retreated back along the riverbank.

"Goodbye, Hannah," Bo called over his shoulder, and then he was gone.

"How long?" Sayid asked Hannah. "And don't pretend you don't know what I'm asking."

"It depends on how quickly his body starts to reject the foreign bacteria," Hannah said, still looking down the trail. She felt a tear blaze a path down her cheek.

"How. Long?" he repeated.

"He will probably start feeling sick tonight. He could be sick for weeks."

"Only sick?"

"At the very least. I really don't know what's going to happen to him." She turned to look him in the eyes. "If he dies, so help me…"

"What? You are going to kill me?" Sayid said. "If I hadn't been so careful to avoid death and recognize a down another cruel blow on her head. The men porting her were not careful to avoid dragging the net when they got tired, and occasionally, when the trail descended down a steep hill, rocks and roots would bang against her backside. She couldn't help but think her plight was hopeless. She had been trying for some time to loosen the band around her wrists, but had only succeeded in making her wrists raw from the friction.

When the day turned to night, she started looking forward to them halting their progress and making camp for the night. It would be a small relief, as she would still be their captive, but she needed a rest from the constant pain inflicted by their journey.

She kept glancing back at the soul eater behind her, who seemed to be staring at her intensely anytime she turned around. It was unnerving how he seemed to be able to see her without the aid of eyes. His footing was sure on the uneven trail, perhaps even more sure than those who carried her. They hadn't sewn their eyelids closed, but it was apparent that the dimming light was slowing their progress.

She thought she might try to sleep, however uncomfortable she was, and as she closed her eyes, she poorly-planned attempt on my life, I might be frightened." He leaned forward, getting uncomfortably close to Hannah, and spoke in a quiet, calm voice. "There's a reason I made it onto the ship and 99.9 percent of the human population did not. I know how to survive. I have also saved Salman from assassination attempts multiple times. You could fill a cemetery with the bodies of those who tried to outlive me. If you think you can be the lucky one to take my life, you are welcome to try. But it will cost you exactly one life."

Hannah could visualize where his gun was holstered on his hip, and wondered if she could draw it before he could. She did not remove her eyes from his. She might never get another chance as good as this. *He was so close!*

"Sayid!" a voice called from the jungle. Sayid stood and Hannah could see he already had a hand on his pistol. He must have been baiting her to try to get to it. She had literally dodged a bullet. She let herself breathe.

"What is it, Li?" When Sayid stepped away, Hannah allowed herself to look. Li was running toward them, alone.

"He's dead! Bo is dead!"

VIII

Giant clouds were visible in the far distance, but they did not look like storm clouds. They were ashen in color, similar to a volcano. Kit determined they had originated from the nearest metropolis, New London, but she wasn't aware of any active volcanoes in that area. It was far enough away that she hadn't heard any rumblings to indicate anything had happened before they reached this pinnacle overlooking the jungle trees. The Lamek warriors each drew a sharp blade across their palms and smeared sanguine streaks of blood across their chests. They seemed to be celebrating whatever cataclysmic event had just happened. Before Kit could muster up the courage to ask anything, they hoisted her up and continued their journey back into the trees.

Kit shifted in the net, trying to find comfort in another position. Maneuvering in the net was difficult to do, and she feared rocking the net too much and bringing

11

I thought he said I wouldn't be able to speak, Donovan
said, breaking his scared silence.

Is what you're doing speaking? came a voice in return.
Is anyone's mouth moving to project your words into the air?

The sensation was so strange. He was still alive
and moving around, but he had no control of his actions.
He saw through Hugh's eyes, took in the breath from
Hugh's nostrils, even tasted the flavors of the foods Hugh
ate. It *felt* like it was him doing all these things, but
Donovan knew he was not piloting this body. He had
about as much control over this body as he did over the
weather. He could sense a rainfall, but he couldn't change
it to sunshine.

*If I could speak, I could say things in just about every
language,* Donovan observed.

That's because many of us know different languages,
someone said in a different tongue. Donovan could
understand what he was saying, even though he had never

back in the pod, lying on the floor. Joshua was kneeling next to her, holding a needle attached to rubber tubing. The full weight of mortality hit her like a boulder, and all her physical aches and pains felt magnified with every movement. Her right hand especially hurt.

"Ow-w-w!" she said, looking down at the back of her hand which now resembled a pincushion. "What happened to my hand?"

Joshua hid the tubing behind his back.

learned how to speak that language in life.

So why can't I control his body? he asked. *Why can't any of us?*

He's far stronger than all of us combined. You think we haven't tried?

How many of "us" are there? Donovan asked.

Thousands. Hugh has been doing this for a long time. Into Donovan's memory came the judgment of thousands of men, each justified when they attempted to rob someone of life. They came to him as if they were his own memories.

How old is Hugh? Donovan asked. *I have none of his memories. I only can recall those you all have of him. Many of them go back thousands of years!*

If we knew his age, you would also. As for Hugh's memories, you will never be able to think his thoughts. A weaker man you would be able to draw memories, behaviors, mannerisms, and language from; basically, take over his life. But not Hugh. Like we said, he is far too strong for any of us to break through.

That's because none of you are royalty, Donovan said. They all laughed.

You forget, we have your memories too, usurper. He suppresses us and only sets us free on a tether when he has use for us.

recalled that Xrys was Lamek by birth, and was only adopted by the Tutek after they saved him from being sacrificed at birth.

"So if everything has a spirit, that would mean that rocks and dirt are…" she paused as realization set in.

"Alive?" Xrys finished for her.

Marai now knew why she felt a spiritual connection to the planet when she removed her shoes and walked barefoot: Mother Hope was a living being! She was overcome with the thought of being so connected to everything around her, to know they shared a creator, and she was filled with feelings of peace and hope, unlike anything she had ever felt before. She was just beginning to understand the true nature of everything, and it was as sweet and warm as bathing in sunlight.

Suddenly, the trees began to spin. She dropped to her knees to stop the movement.

"You have been away too long!" Xrys said. "I can continue to look for Kit. You must get back to One-Who-Saves."

"Joshua," she told him.

"You're awake!" Joshua said.

Marai opened her physical eyes and saw herself

You will meet Tai and Borghaus soon enough and they can share with you how that goes.

Donovan changed the subject. *Where does he get his ability to take a life without using weapons? How can he keep us captive inside himself?*

We believe his friend Jack gives him this power. He sometimes will use us to squeeze the life out of men's hearts if they outnumber him, as you so unfortunately witnessed.

He took your life, said one. *He always takes the leader.*

Who is Jack? Donovan asked.

Nobody knows. Sure enough, Donovan could sense about as many theories concerning Jack as there were individuals. He knew that Jack existed outside of Hugh, and that Hugh could see him only when he looked in a reflective surface. Strangely enough, even though they all saw through Hugh's eyes, nobody seemed to be able to see Jack when Hugh spoke to him. They just knew he carried on many conversations with him.

It was a lot to take in all in one day. Not to mention the fact that Donovan hadn't yet come to terms with the fact that he had died earlier that morning.

You're going to miss your own funeral.

Donovan watched through Hugh's eyes as he sat

you spirit walk, the weaker your body and spirit become. We must find your mother!"

"Can I not ask one of the living?" Marai asked.

"You are still connected to the physical realm, since your body still lives. If one of them had your gift, you could speak to him, but I'm afraid none of them could ever see me when I spirit walked in life. Just as I cannot see them now."

"You cannot see them?"

"Yes, I have no physical eyes with which to perceive the physical world. You still have both, so you can."

"But… if you cannot perceive physical things, how can you see the trees, water, and land but not the people living on it?"

"Because the trees, water, and land have spirits. The Creator made all things spiritually before he clothed them in flesh."

"Aren't *people* spirits clothed in flesh?"

"Yes, but for some reason, we can only see those whom we have a physical connection with. Those with whom we are tied together by blood. I can even *feel* their presence without having to see them." Xrys said. Marai in the car with the reigns in his hands. Donovan's hands, but not Donovan's hands.

This is going to be hard to get used to.

Hugh slept easy that night, but Donovan stayed awake. He felt Hugh's need to rest, as if it were his own need, but he was determined to escape. He pushed his way upward, trying to break through into Hugh's head.

Open your eyes. Open them up!

Donovan tried to open his eyes, just as he would have before his "death," but his body would not respond to his commands.

Come on, how hard can it be to open my eyes?!

Those aren't your eyes, a voice answered.

They feel like my eyes! Donovan responded. He tried to lift his hands—which he could *clearly* feel resting on his chest—to his head to open his eyelids manually. His hands didn't respond.

Those aren't your hands, either.

Shut up! Donovan screamed. *I can feel them right there! If I can feel them, then surely I can move them!*

You're welcome to keep trying, the voice responded.

Kit was not in the village. Marai couldn't find her in any of the huts or among the warriors who were holding a mass funeral for their departed tribal family. Large holes had been dug at the base of the Sacred mountain, and the bodies of the deceased were lovingly placed therein according to family; mothers, fathers and children arranged in a loving embrace before having a blanket of earth covering their final resting place. Of course, Marai could see the spirits of the dead looking on, crying for the mourning of those left behind.

By himself in a small hole, lay the crippled body of Xrys. Marai stood next to him as he watched his burial. She slipped her hand into his to show her support.

"It might not have been the most agile body, but it was mine," he said.

"I am so sorry, Xrys!"

"I will be fine." he said. "Death is not the end of life."

Marai felt her hand pass through his. She held it up, and saw that it didn't glow as brightly as it did earlier that day. She could even see through herself. Xrys looked at her and must have seen concern on her face.

"You are weakening. The further and the longer

Donovan tried to move again. Then he tried flexing the muscles in his arms; *any* muscles.

Nothing moved.

It was a prison of the strangest making. He felt enveloped in blackness, and the blackness held him paralyzed. For a moment, he thought maybe Hugh had died in his sleep, but then he felt his chest rising and falling, felt his lungs filling with the cool night air.

Just open my bloody eyes!! If there's a deity in heaven, please hear me and help me!

Suddenly Donovan could see the embers of a campfire and two horses tied to a tree. His eyes were open.

It worked! I am in control! I took his body over while he slept!

Donovan decided to speak out loud.

"What would you like me to say?"

Wait… those aren't the words I wanted to speak.

"That's because they *aren't* your words," Hugh said. "They're mine."

But… I opened my eyes.

"Actually, I opened *my* eyes," Hugh said. "You have never been—nor ever will be—in control of this body. It belongs to me and nobody else. You only have as relative of this fish in her bowl at home when she was younger. It passed by without acknowledging her floating there, although she couldn't be sure with the absent stare if it had seen her or not. But having seen it and put a face to her fear, she could see that it was just another beautiful creation living out its life in the crystal-clear water of the lake.

I have nothing to worry about, she thought.

You are safe, Xrys answered.

Marai started to feel herself move through the water toward the far shore. When they emerged onto the shore, she turned around, took a few steps, and tried to stand on the surface of the water again. It bore her weight.

"I don't fear the deep anymore," Marai said, proudly.

"Good!" Xrys said. "I am just glad the lake monster that swam past was not the *really* large kind with sharp teeth."

Marai sunk into the water a little, then scrambled to shore.

Xrys just laughed.

much control as I allow you to have, and I'm not about to give that up to the likes of you or anyone."

I thought that maybe while you slept…

"You thought wrong. Just because I sleep doesn't mean I give up my agency."

What does agency have to do with anything?

"As long as I choose to exercise judgment righteously, I have power over those who do not. It has fallen on my shoulders to protect humankind against themselves, especially when it comes to the taking of another's life unjustly. That doesn't change simply because I slumber."

Was that you I was speaking to tonight?

"Yes."

I wondered about that. I couldn't share your thoughts.

"That's because this is my brain, and you don't have the key to unlock it."

What would happen if I did?

"Then I suppose you would take over the functions of my body. You would be the one in control."

And I could tap into your thoughts and memories as you have mine?

"I suppose so. You could do a pretty good

anyway.

Yes, there are. Xrys said.

As if in response to his words, a large, dark shadow passed directly underneath her.

There are lake monsters!! Xrys, I cannot be courageous when there are lake monsters!

Courage is not absence of fear. It is faith in the face of fear. You will always have fear of the unknown, but let me rest your mind a little. Yes, these 'lake monsters,' as you call them, are large enough to swallow a man whole, but what have you to fear of that, in your current state?

Marai thought about that for a minute. She was spirit matter now, and could probably pass through a lake monster as she could through any other solid matter.

…and it probably cannot see you, anyway, Xrys added to her thought.

Probably?

Xrys didn't answer that thought. Just let her think it through.

Another lake monster swam past, this time near enough she could make out details in the dark. It just looked like a large fish. It had long, flowing fins and an almost kind look in its eye. She may have had a smaller impersonation of me, so that even my own mother wouldn't know it's not me."

So then why don't you let me have a turn at the wheel? Give me the key so I can drive for a while?

"Not going to happen, Donovan."

Why not?

"Because I don't aspire to lead a ragtag group of miscreants around committing petit theft for the rest of my life."

Royalty has its perks!

"I'll ask a queen, next time I meet one."

If you won't let me live a free life, then why don't you just release me?

"Believe me, what I am doing is merciful. If I untether you, you'll wander the planet as a lost soul, mourning for the sensation of a warm touch, the taste of good food, and the breathing of fresh air. Having a body is the only way you experience that, even if it's my body."

For now.

"Sure. You just keep telling yourself that," Hugh said. "Now I'm going to close my own eyes, and get some sleep."

Donovan's eyes closed, and Hugh slept.

is only when you walked on the surface of water that you began to doubt what was actually happening. Your thoughts began to rob you of belief, and your lack of belief robbed you of power.

Try to move forward in the water without moving, Xrys said. *Ask the water to move you where you want to go.*

Marai envisioned being whisked though the water to the far shore, and away from the mysterious blackness underneath her. She didn't seem to be moving.

Marai, you need to let go of my hand.

Marai released her grip on Xrys' hand and tried to have the water move her forward again. She only seemed to sink further. The light from the surface started to dim as she went down.

Xrys, what am I doing wrong? She asked.

He sank down to her level and spoke to her without taking her hand.

You still have fear. Fear is the opposite of faith. The Destroyer wants you to fear. Let yourself sink so that you may see there is nothing to fear.

Marai tried to cast away years of irrational fear. She couldn't help but be scared, even though the deepest thing she had ever swam in was a swimming pool in the city, and there were no such things as lake monsters,

12

Apparently, the reaction Bo had with the water was deadly. Hannah speculated that it might have been the large amount of water—and conversely, foreign bacteria—that ultimately ended her friend's life so suddenly. Maybe small amounts of water at a time could be introduced into their systems and they could slowly build up an immunity?

Or maybe not. She didn't know anything, except her friend was dead and her chances of ever escaping were diminishing. If what Sayid said about him being a survivor was true, it would be next to impossible to get the better of him. How do you catch a person like that unaware? She would have to recognize an opportunity before he did, which might be asking too much.

"Did you manage to bring anything back?" Sayid asked Li.

"No," Li said. "We didn't make it that far. Bo started vomiting blood about one hundred yards down the

WOOD/LIFEBLOOD

Do not worry, you cannot drown, Xrys' voice sounded inside her head. She looked behind her and saw Xrys floating peacefully, holding her hand. *Your desire to breathe is only in your head. You have no lungs to fill while in this state.*

Marai let herself relax and realized that she didn't have any burning sensation in her chest as she hovered, completely immersed. *I can't move forward,* Marai thought. *I saw you leaving me behind and I started sinking.*

You stopped believing.

Okay. So what do I need to do now? she asked.

You are still relying on yourself to do all the work rather than allow creation to carry you. When you walk on the earth in body, you may push off it with your foot, but it also pushes back against you to propel you forward. While in spirit, you must ask the earth, wind, and water to do the pushing for you. Believe that the Creator made all things to work in harmony with His children. His children are the lifeblood of this planet. In this lightened state, your spirit can pass through the matter around it, so you must enlist its help to carry you.

So why did I not sink into the ground the first time I walked in spirit? Marai asked.

You had no reason to believe it would not hold you up, Xrys said. *It had held you up for your entire lifetime before that. It* trail."

"Take your E-tool and go bury him," Sayid said.

"Bury him?" Li asked.

"YES, BURY HIM!" Sayid shouted.

"Aye, sir," Li said, then took his tool out of his pack and went off down the trail.

Hannah decided to occupy her mind with something else while Li was away giving Bo a hasty funeral. She wandered around the campsite Kent had made, admiring his little garden for the first attempt to introduce Earth-compatible food. She went into Kent's hut in the tree and looked around, making sure to stay visible to Sayid through the entrance so as not to arouse suspicion. She was impressed with the construction of the hut. Kent must have had some experience with building, because there was a semi-level floor, walls, and a roof frame over which was stretched his parachute for protection against the weather. His bedding still lay on the floor, which was a good sign he would be coming back soon. Next to his bedding on the floor was a photo of two men wearing suits at what looked like a cemetery. Hannah assumed the muscular one was Kent and the other looked like a brother; similar in look, but much thinner. They both penetrated the surface of the lake deeper, and she didn't move very far forward before stopping completely. She started sinking lower and lower into the lake's surface. She felt panic arise in her, and desperately began thrashing her legs and then her arms in an attempt to "swim" forward, but she wasn't moving at all now.

Before her head went under, she shouted for Xrys to help her, but she couldn't see him anymore, and feared he had gone too far. She called out in her mind, knowing Xrys could communicate with her using thoughts.

Xrys, where are you? I'm sinking and I don't know how to get across the lake anymore!

Xrys!?

He didn't answer. Her head was now completely underwater and she dared not breathe in, in case her spirit could still drown. All she could see was blackness below her, and her thoughts started to conjure up all sorts of lake monsters that were swimming below her, and she began to be terrified.

Xrys!!

Suddenly, something grabbed her hand from behind. She screamed without meaning to. Then panicked that she would run out of breath underwater.

were smiling with their arms around one another. They looked happy, even though the circumstances must have been sad at the time.

How many of us have had to leave loved ones behind?

She lay down on the bedding and drifted off.

It was really dark by the time Li came back to the camp, tired and hungry. Sayid had made a fire and was cooking something in a mess-kit pot from his pack. He sat down next to Sayid without speaking, removed his pack, and laid his rifle across the top of it. He opened his pack, pulled out a Meal-Ready-to-Eat, opened it, and began to eat it cold.

"I grabbed two sleeping bags from the pod," he said between bites. "I figured one of us would always be on watch tonight."

"Good," Sayid said. "I will take first watch."

"Thank you, sir," Li said. He realized the girl was not around. "Where's Hannah?"

"She's asleep in the hut," Sayid answered.

"Should I wake her up to eat?"

"Let her sleep," Sayid said. "I don't want to have

bore her weight.

"Your spirit self is far less dense than your body. The water will bear you up if you allow it to," Xrys said. "Push off with your feet."

She propelled herself forward and glided over the water as she had over the rainforest floor. Her flight was smooth, and she figured this was due to her spirit self having far fewer molecules to collide with air particles and slow her down. She took a few more steps, and looked up to see if Xrys was still ahead of her. He was sailing about thirty yards ahead of her and she noticed how much faster he seemed to move than she did. The distance seemed to grow with every second and she started to worry about him leaving her. She thrust her foot down into the water and tried to propel herself faster, but noticed that her foot had broken the surface of the water. It wasn't wet, but she was surprised that the dense molecules of water had stopped supporting her less-dense spirit molecules. She looked up once again and saw Xrys was now a tiny speck on the surface of the large lake. She looked behind her and noticed that she had probably traveled far enough that she was near the middle of the lake.

She tried to push off with her other foot, but it

to deal with her anymore tonight."

Li still got up and made a visual confirmation that Hannah was in the tree house. He didn't want Sayid blaming *him* if she had already escaped. He went back and got his sleeping bag, then took it into the treehouse and lay down on the floor below Hannah's feet. She stirred a little, but went back to sleep.

Li felt sorry for her. She hadn't chosen this life. Nor was she built to handle this sort of lifestyle. Li had seen enough men die—some at his own hands—that death didn't affect him like it did her. She was a scientist. She should be in a climate-controlled lab looking at cultures in a petri dish under a microscope, not out in the jungle with a psychopathic, paranoid gunslinger.

Li *had* chosen this life, even though he didn't always agree with the missions his superior officers in the SF gave him. He only obeyed the orders of Sayid because he didn't believe in making trouble for himself. In an army of two-and-a-quarter million back home in China, he found it easier to just blend in. Despite all his effort, he was recognized for his hand-to-hand combat skills, and made a personal bodyguard to the Minister of National Defense, who was a part of the Secret Council on Earth.

social skills it is, then. It seems like a small price to pay to be able to move the way I want.

Joshua closed his eyes and began to repair his damaged brain.

Marai and Xrys came to the lake above the waterfall, and Xrys left the trail and started to float over the water, every once in a while putting down a foot to propel himself. Marai stopped at the shore and Xrys looked back after noticing she was not beside him.

"Why do you hesitate?" he asked.

"I just… I did not think we would be crossing over water."

"This is the shortest path to the village."

Marai knew Xrys was right, as the trail on the far side of the lake went all the way to the base of the mountain before the water was narrow enough to cross (and even then, it was over a bridge). Still, it just felt weird to cross over a surface she knew would swallow her while in body.

"Do not hesitate. Only believe."

She stepped out onto the water, and felt that it

Here again, he made it his policy to go along peacefully. He was young and had no family to leave behind, so it made little difference to him *where* he served.

Now Earth was gone. He had the opportunity to retire from military life and settle down on a planet with a future. If he could just get through his service in the upcoming war on the people of this planet, he could finally lay this lifestyle to rest.

He fell asleep, dreaming of a house with a fence.

Hannah awoke in the middle of the night when she heard Sayid call out.

"Who is there?" he shouted.

"It's me, Kent Waller!" a voice came from the trees. "Don't shoot, sir!"

Hannah emerged from the hut with Li, who had apparently fallen asleep in there also. Kent walked into the firelight with his hands raised. He *was* the person in the photo. Sayid holstered his gun while Hannah and Li climbed down to join them.

"Is the boy with you?" Sayid asked.

"Interesting story," Kent said, sitting down and

was never complete. Joshua still had his entire brain, but he realized he might have to sacrifice some brain functions in order to re-learn others. He went back inside himself and evaluated his current situation. His long-term memory was damaged; he was only able to recall bits of his past. His motor skills were shot. He had significant damage to his left hemisphere, because his verbal skills were gone. But his reasoning was still intact, as was his spatial perception.

What would I be willing to part with in order to gain control over my body? My long-term memory doesn't seem so important now, but that's probably because I can't remember what is <u>so</u> <u>important</u> to remember! Would sacrificing this be so bad if I never knew what I am supposed to miss? Maybe there's important information stored there that I would be foolish to let go.

What about my social skills? All of the training I've had by associating with others and being taught the rules of society? Those don't seem to be very important in a world where I would rather be left alone. And who's to say what "normal" behavior should look like anyway? Weren't there plenty of variations from culture to culture of what constituted "normalcy?" And perhaps I can relearn these skills according to Marai's culture at some future date? Retrieving my memories once they're gone would not be possible. So picking through the discarded MRE bag. "Did you know there's *people* on this planet?"

"Yes," Sayid said. "Is the boy with you?"

"In answer to your question: No," Kent said. "But I know where he is. Did someone eat the pound cake out of here?"

"Where is he?" Sayid said, ignoring Kent's question.

"Hold your horses, sir," Kent said. "With all due respect, of course. I don't think they're going to stay where they are now. I have reason to believe they'll be on the move in a few days. But I know where they will be headed. We can beat them there. Is there another MRE around here? I'm starving!"

"*Them?*" Li asked, tossing him an MRE out of his pack.

"Oh, yeah… He's traveling with a girl named Marai," Kent said. "Potatoes au gratin! I'd rather eat my weeds."

Li gestured for him to give it back. "Just kidding, I'll eat it," Kent said. He opened it and started tearing into the contents.

"Can I have your heater?" Hannah asked. "I'm

into this state, but if it was to continue, she was going to need fluids in her body. After struggling with the needle for an hour, he fell back against the bulkhead, exhausted.

Why can't I do this? What do I need to do to recover the things I've lost?

As Joshua reflected on his current state of helplessness, he started to recall some of the medical readings he had perused during his years on the ship from Earth. There was one procedure, in particular, which now came to the forefront of his mind.

Back on Earth, there had been a woman who was suffering from epileptic seizures to the point where her quality of life was completely ruined. In order to save her life, she agreed to have a brain surgeon try an experimental new procedure called a hemispherectomy, where the damaged hemisphere of her brain would be completely removed. After the surgery, her remaining hemisphere started learning to perform tasks which were normally performed by the other side of her brain. The seizures were gone, and she learned how to live with half of a brain.

She reassigned her brain functions!

The trade-off of stopping the seizures was not without a price, though. She lived, but her quality of life freezing!" Only then did Kent seem to notice her.

"You brought me a girlfriend too, Sayid?" Kent said. "How thoughtful!" He winked at her and tossed his MRE heater to her.

Li opened his canteen and poured a little water into Hannah's heater bag. "Just shake it up a little and the water will start to work with the chemicals to create heat," Li said.

"I know how an MRE heater works," Hannah said. "I've watched you use them before."

Kent made an agitated cat noise. "A little testy, are we? The man was just trying to help!"

Hannah tucked the heater into the front of her jacket and held it there with both hands.

"Where will they be?" Sayid asked, leaning forward into Kent's space.

Kent swallowed a mouthful of food and answered, "They'll probably be heading to a village near a cliff wall back up the trail and to the left. It's not very far from here."

"Then we should go at once," Sayid said, standing and preparing to put on his pack. "Let's get to the pod."

"What, now?" Kent said. "I just got here!"

she was here."

"*While* she was here?" Marai was relieved to know her mother had been here and made it out alive, but she still didn't know how Xrys knew this.

"These are the tracks of my people," Xrys said, as if in response to her thought. "They encircled your mom facing outward while she searched. They were protecting her."

Marai didn't know Xrys knew how to track people. She started to have hope. "Where do the tracks lead from here?"

"Back to the village."

Joshua struggled to make his hands work the way he needed them to. It was a simple task, one he had done to himself many times when he went into stasis on the voyage. Put the clamp on the hose, hang the bag on the hook, and insert the needle into her vein. But he had no fine motor skills, and he might as well be performing in a ballet as trying to save Marai's life.

She needed him. She had lapsed into a coma and was completely unresponsive. He wasn't sure how she fell

Hannah took the moment Sayid looked back to insert his arm into the other strap of his pack to throw her makeshift bomb. She had tied the top of the MRE heater bag inside of her coat and it had begun to expand rapidly. It wouldn't do anything but make a loud noise, but she didn't need it to do much more than that. It landed in-between the three men and exploded with a deafening pop.

She had Li's rifle pointed at Sayid's head before he could react.

"This is where I say goodbye," she told Sayid.

Two rapid gunshots rang out, and Hannah fell down with holes in her chest.

"You should have just pulled the trigger," Sayid said. "Goodbye, then."

He put one more bullet in her head.

WOOD/LIFEBLOOD

It was so good to see him again! She hugged him once more, then pulled away quickly when she remembered why she was spirit walking.

"Have you seen my mother?" Marai asked.

"Living people are obscured from my view. All I know is that she left the village on the night of the massacre, which is what you know."

"Will you walk with me while I look for her?" Marai asked.

"Walk?" Xrys levitated a few feet off the ground. "Marai, you still have much to learn about your spirit self."

There were signs that someone had been to the cab, but Marai wasn't sure if it was her mother or whomever had scattered their belongings and burned the cab interior. Marai just hoped their arrival hadn't been simultaneous.

"There are no arrows," Xrys said.

"Do you think someone picked them up?" Marai asked.

"Most likely. Spent arrows are still useful. But what I am saying is, nobody attacked your mother while

13

A burnt-out cab rested against a hill on the mountain road.

"I bet my people do this, boss," Tai said. "This they type of arrow."

"Where do the tracks go from here?" Hugh asked.

"There plenty of tracks, some go toward the lake, some go off into the trees. Why you think this matter? This don't look like a spaceship to me. We already see the dead cabbie down the road. Case closed."

"There were others in this car," Hugh said.

"How you know that?" Tai asked.

"Because it's a cab, you moron," Borghaus said.

"Oh," Tai said. "So what, we going to chase them down and make sure they pay the fare?"

"Are you in a hurry to get somewhere?" Hugh asked, as he used a stick to lift some burned electronics. "I don't know *what* I'm looking for, and may not know until I

"What has happened to him?" Xrys asked.

"I think he has had a terrible reaction to the water on our planet," Marai said. "I think it almost killed him, but I have reason to believe he is recovering."

"I never thought the Eternal One would be so… mortal," Xrys said.

"I am worried, Xrys. He probably will never be the same. Are you sure he is the one I was supposed to meet? He knows nothing about any prophecy or… what we are supposed to do from here."

"I cannot know for sure," Xrys said. "My window into the mortal world is limited. I only see small visions through your eyes because of our spiritual connection. I believe he is the one, but I was never a seer or prophet."

"Well, neither am I," Marai said. "It sure would be nice if someone could just tell me what to do."

"There is little growth in that," Xrys said. "We are given many paths to choose from, but the choice—and its consequences—will be ours alone."

"*You* sound like a prophet," Marai said. "I will just take your advice and blame the consequences on you."

"Then I refuse to give you any more advice," Xrys said with a smile.

find it."

Hugh prided himself in being able to read a story from a crime scene. The arrow was protruding from a tire, and must have been the reason why the cab had stopped here and been pushed off the road. This was a narrow road, only wide enough for one vehicle, with a mountain rising up on one side and a forested drop-off on the other. He didn't find any spare tires, which could explain why the cabbie was found down the road going back to the city. A similar arrow had ended his life. He hadn't gotten very far, which meant the passengers of the cab must have been attacked shortly after.

"Tai," Hugh said, "where are you seeing tracks that go off the side of the cliff?"

"I don't see tracks, boss," Tai answered. "Come look at the edge of the road. The ground broken off here, like someone run off this way."

"How many people? Can you tell?"

"There two paths down there through the grass."

"I don't see two paths."

"It can be hard to see. Look for where the grass is shorter, because someone pulled it up running. See?"

Hugh squatted down like Tai was doing and could

wasn't even sure what she was doing was walking, really, since she didn't really have a body to speak of. In her fear of what had become of her mom, she had decided that morning to leave Joshua sleeping and go see if there were any signs of her mom's whereabouts.

To leave her body and "spirit walk," as Xrys had called it, she had to lie still in a state of meditation and let go of all her bodily connections. She had to abandon her reliance on her physical senses and completely trust in her feelings. She was still connected to her body, but the further she separated from her body, the weaker her spirit became. This was mostly in the form of confusion of thought, because physical fatigue didn't exist while she was in this state.

"You have found him," a familiar voice said from behind her.

"Xrys!" She turned around and her friend whom she hadn't seen since his physical death gathered her into an embrace. It still caught her off guard that she could feel his touch while in spirit form. Since she could only perceive the spirits of the deceased after she removed the veil of her physical eyes, it was a delight to see he was nearby.

barely make out a difference in the height of the undergrowth in two paths.

"Okay, I think I can see them," Hugh said. "I think these were the passengers from the cab who escaped, then a large group came to the cab later, maybe to scavenge and set the cab on fire."

"The cab set on fire before the group get here," Tai said.

"How do you know that?" Hugh asked.

"My dead brother tell me."

Hugh had forgotten momentarily that Tai was between worlds, and could see the spirits of the deceased. Apparently, one of his people was nearby, and Tai chose *now* to tell him. "What else can he tell us about the people from this car?" Hugh asked.

Tai looked off to the side and said something in a strange tongue. "Only that he chase them and he get killed near a waterfall."

"Who were they chasing?"

Another pause for conversation. "The Seer, he say. The Destroyer want her dead, along with someone he call the Wretched One."

"I don't like this guy," Borghaus said. "He keeps

WOOD/LIFEBLOOD

movements would land him back on the pillow. He regretted ever taking for granted not having to think about moving.

After a long, laborious rise which seemed to take an eternity, Joshua was sitting up with his feet on the floor. He looked at Marai lying on her back and the panic set in again. In his haste, he tried to stand and fell forward, only *just* gaining enough control of his body to catch himself on his hands and knees. He looked up and started inching toward Marai, one limb at a time.

"Marai. Marai!"

She still didn't move.

Joshua finally reached her side and bent over to listen and look for breathing. He barely caught his head before he crashed into her nose. A slight tickle of air touched his cheek, and he could hear her breathing coming regularly. He felt the panic loosen its grip on his mind. Marai was alive.

Still, he was left with a burning question in his mind: What had happened to Marai?

Marai walked lightly on the forest floor. She

testing you to see if he can enter your body, Hugh."

"I try to tell him it is useless," Tai said.

"Who's this 'Wretched One?'" Hugh asked. "Find out more about that."

"He tell me he come from the sky. He must be destroyed."

"He came from the sky, huh? In a spaceship?"

"We no have word for 'spaceship,' boss."

"Then explain it in a different way."

Tai took a few moments, trying to describe a flying vehicle in a foreign tongue. Hugh could see he was really struggling, but he figured if Tai's invisible friend had seen something like that, it would have left an impression.

"Yes, and another one a few days ago," Tai finally said. "He tell us the Wretched One and girl together bring the end of the world."

In the far recesses of his mind, Hugh remembered his father speaking of drawings in a cave that predicted the end of the world. This was many lifetimes ago so the memory was vague, but he did seem to recall two people being involved.

What was most troubling, though was the way this dead warrior spoke of it as if it was near. Hugh knew they

VII

Marai wouldn't wake up. Joshua kept calling her name from his bed, but she didn't stir from her prostrate position on the floor. He began to be very anxious.

"Marai, Marai, Marai…" Joshua found himself repeating her name over and over, despite wanting to say more. It was as if he was stuck in automatic mode and couldn't turn it off. Soon, it became too much for him to bear. He had to try to get out of bed and go check on her. He struggled to control his body. His fine motor skills had been lost in the infection, along with many other precious brain connections. He didn't have time to wonder if they would ever come back, because only one thought kept occupying his mind.

Marai is dead.

He struggled to sit up. It was almost like he had to re-learn how to move. He actually had to concentrate on which limb to move and how, or else sudden, jerky worshipped death and destruction, and if they were convinced these two were the same two which heralded the end, perhaps there was something to it.

Hugh thought back on the last few weeks and got a sinking feeling in the pit of his stomach. Before any bomb was dropped, before any city was destroyed, people responded to the power outage differently than he had ever witnessed. They *felt* like it was the end of the world. Of course, the world being on the brink of war in the years leading up to these most recent events might have had something to do with it, but Hugh had to admit that he had been feeling the same way too.

That's why he was here.

"Hugh, we might want to get moving," Borghaus said, snapping him back to the present. "There's more of Tai's friends around us now, and it's getting pretty uncomfortable."

"Speak of the devil…" Hugh said, mostly to himself. Then to Tai he said, "We need to find out which direction the Visitors went."

"They not answer anymore, Boss," Tai said.

"They're starting to chant something," Borghaus said nervously. As he spoke, a fiery explosion lit up the always mean causation, it seemed more likely than not that lack of scientific understanding and reasoning usually meant more bogeymen and fairies.

She had her personally held beliefs, but had to admit they were more wishful thinking than anything. The loss of her husband in a random shooting years before had given her cause to wish for a life after death, but the more she studied, the less she seemed to believe. She had occasionally prayed to God, when desperation called for it, but her prayers never seemed to be answered. Her current situation only helped solidify that belief. She had pleaded to God to help her find her daughter safe, and she still had no idea of Marai's whereabouts. To make matters worse, "God" had allowed her to be ensnared by a murderous tribe, taking away her ability to look for her daughter.

His refusal to listen to her most heartfelt prayers was more evidence of the natural state of her being. Humans just *were*. Life just *happened*. Then they *weren't* anymore. Simple. *A lot of good belief in a creator had done the Tutek people!* She had a grim idea of how this would all end. If she couldn't escape this mess using her own critical faculties, no god was going to intervene on her behalf. It started to rain, and she started to plan.

trees off the edge of the road.

"That maybe be from a spaceship," Tai said. "Maybe we no need to ask."

"It was about three miles away," Borghaus observed.

"We're going to have to go off-road," Hugh said. He quickly unhitched Babe and threw the blanket and saddle from the car over her back, securing it. Then he tied Dusty's reins to her saddle and mounted. "You ready for this, girl?" he asked Babe, patting her neck. He knew this had been a longer than average day for her. Hugh had kept going into the night, anticipating setting up camp next to the lake with the mountain in-view. Now he was asking her to carry him another three miles through steep and rough terrain.

"Hya!"

Hugh leaned back in the saddle and Babe picked her way down the steep hill between the trees. Hugh feared some of the larger leaves covering the ground would cause her to slip, but she stayed sure all the way down into the canyon. Dusty kept pace with her, snorting all the way down.

Hugh looked back and saw that Tai and Borghaus

who lived so differently than she, but these last few weeks, seeing the atrocities committed at their hands firsthand, she now felt a deep, abiding contempt for them. They had slaughtered the people she loved in their sleep, and now were intent on finding her daughter. For what purpose? All she knew now, staring into the shriveled eyes of the soul hunter, was that she would do anything in her power to protect her daughter, even if that meant disrupting a way of life she had vowed as an anthropologist to protect.

"You will not lay a finger on my daughter," she said fiercely.

The soul eater tilted his head back and laughed. "You have not the power to stop us. We are guided by The Destroyer." He looked back. It was uncanny how he seemed to stare without eyes.

Of course, the things they believed were products of an uncivilized people who didn't have science to give them observable phenomena to take the place of superstition. She would have never said as much to any of her classes, but in her observations, the simpler the way-of-life, the greater the belief in gods, witchcraft, and spirits. There was a direct correlation between less education and more superstition, and while she knew correlation didn't had opted to jump onto Dusty's back rather than be towed along by their tethers. It was just as well. They weakened when they got too far from him, and he needed them to be strong.

They came to a river, and Hugh noticed a trail that sometimes followed the river's winding course. The trail seemed to be going in the direction the explosion came from, so he followed it downriver.

They came to a campsite near the river along the way. Next to the smoldering fire lay the body of a woman. Hugh crouched next to her and felt a terrible unbalance in the air. She had been shot three times, and then left where she had fallen. Something about her felt… familiar.

Hugh looked around until he found a sleeping bag in a nearby treehouse. He unzipped it and spread it over the top of her. He took off his hat and held it over his heart.

"Sorry you were taken unjustly," Hugh said. He replaced his hat, mounted his horse, and started back down the trail in the direction of the smoke.

"She say she proud of you, boss," Tai said.

Hugh noticed another unbalanced feeling further down the trail, he looked around and noticed a hastily dug

Kit knew he spoke of The Destroyer. She had made a lifetime's work studying the indigenous peoples of this country, and she knew that they were very open about their religious beliefs. They were either strong followers of a deity called "The Creator" or a deity called "The Destroyer." It had always baffled her why any tribe would willingly worship a destructive being with a name such as "The Destroyer," until she studied the writings of one of her contemporaries. They equated worship of The Destroyer with power. It wasn't "good vs. evil" in their minds, it was more "weak vs. strong." In their world, where they had to live by their own industry, a weak person was of no value. This carried over into their contempt for the neighboring tribe she had studied among, the Tutek, whom they saw as a disease they needed to rid planet Hope of. There was no room for compassion in their worldview. They threw their disabled infants into the river, they practiced human sacrifice and cannibalism, they plundered others' crops and flocks and then ravaged the land behind them. They regarded anyone as less-than-human who did not worship The Destroyer as they.

Kit had always exercised professionalism and tried not to let ethnocentricity influence her opinion of a people grave just off the trail. There was blood on the ground nearby.

Why would this person get a burial and not the woman?

Hugh continued on until he smelled smoke in the air. He dismounted, tied Babe's reins to a tree, and started walking carefully toward the faint light he could see through the thick trees ahead.

When the light grew brighter, he could see it was coming from what looked like a spaceship that was on fire. The spaceship was in the middle of a rock outcropping, which led Hugh to believe it had landed here before it exploded. Voices could be heard on the other side of the ship, but Hugh couldn't make out what they were saying. He didn't know what caused the explosion, but he didn't want to approach the Visitors who were on the other side, or even risk being exposed to them by leaving the tree line. He wasn't sure if they were friendly, and he wasn't sure he had the ability to judge them if they weren't.

"Go take a look," Hugh told Tai.

"You got it, boss," Tai said. Tai walked with an unhurried swagger toward the ship. Borghaus shook his head, but Hugh noticed he was smiling, ever-so-slightly. After a few moments, Tai returned.

She felt a solid blow to her head and didn't even realize she had been knocked out until she awoke sometime later, this time with wrists, knees, and ankles bound. Her movement was stunted, and she grew angry with her captors.

"What do you want with me?" she yelled. She knew their language was close enough to the Tutek tongue that they would understand her. "Where is my daughter?!"

"Stop!" a voice yelled. The march down an unfamiliar path suddenly stopped, and Kit started to fear what was coming next. She tried to duck her head in case another blow came, but instead, she was dropped heavily on the hard-packed dirt. She opened her eyes and found herself looking at a soul eater bending over her.

"Where *is* your daughter?" he asked.

"I do not know!" Kit hissed. "I was looking for her when you captured me!" Then, a realization hit. "Why are *you* looking for her?"

The man just grinned at her.

"Tell me what you want with my daughter?!" Kit yelled.

"It is not *I* who wants her, but Him whom we serve."

"What did you see?" Hugh asked when he was near.

"The Visitors is people, boss. Just like you and me." Tai said. "But better-looking than this one," he added, pointing to Borghaus. Borghaus didn't take the bait.

"How do you know they were the Visitors?" Hugh asked.

"They wearing clothes with the same logo as the ship," Tai said. "Pretty good detective work, yeah? I get a deputy badge now?"

Hugh just ignored his goading. "What were they talking about?"

"They arguing about something," Tai said. "I didn't listen to what they saying."

"Yeah, real great detective work," Borghaus said.

Tai looked offended. "It didn't last *long!*" Tai said. "One say, 'let's go,' and they leave."

"Follow them," Hugh said. "I will stay back a distance and follow your tether."

"I get weak if you go too far," Tai said.

"We'll stay back a *safe* distance."

"Safe to you or me?" Tai asked.

Hugh just smiled, and Tai took off after them.

VI

Kit struggled to free herself from the net that held her captive. She had been robbed of any means of escape when she was unconscious, apparently. Her pockets were empty, and her pack with all the gear she had recovered was on the back of a Lamek warrior. The netting that held her was too well-made, and she couldn't tear through any of it.

She had observed that the net which held her had been suspended from a pole, being held between two Lamek warriors who marched in the grim procession surrounding her. She tried to swing back and forth with the natural sway of their pacing, hoping to perhaps knock one of them down and gain her freedom. She had estimated there were about thirty warriors and five soul-eaters in this party she would have to outrun if she were able to escape. She grunted as she swung, and the net kept swinging further and further.

14

Sayid was angry.

He was angry that Hannah had attempted to assassinate him twice in one night, even *after* she was dead.

He was angry that Li had been buckled into the copilot's seat when the grenade spoon had dropped onto the floor. He never had a chance.

He was angry at Kent for being so lazy that he wanted to lie down in the first bed he saw, releasing the grenade from underneath the pillow.

He was even angrier that *that moron* had made it out of the ship with him alive. He had almost knocked Sayid over in their mad scramble to escape in four seconds!

He was angry that he hadn't pocketed a box of .45 ammo after he reloaded that morning. He was down to his last three rounds. He could think of three targets he would like to use them on.

snapped his eyes open and looked at her. He tried to speak.

"Marai," he said. He tried to say more, but was having trouble getting his mouth to cooperate. She hugged him and started to cry in earnest.

"Please stay with me, Joshua! I need you! I can't do this alone!"

Joshua tried to raise a hand to pat her on the back, but his body didn't obey. He formed words in his mind to command his hand to raise, but he only succeeded in slightly raising his fingers. He was frightened he might fall into delirium again, but his mental mind-state was different now. He gripped wakefulness with all the strength his mind could muster.

"Marai," he repeated.

She pulled away and wiped her eyes. "Yes?" she answered.

"No… bad… water."

Most of all, he was angry he had lost his transportation back to The Exodus. What were the odds that the grenade fell onto to spot of floor right above the fuel cells? The ship was a complete loss, as he was reminded by the diminishing firelight that illuminated the forest in front of him. He tried to suppress the urge to scream.

He was stranded down here without the means to even *communicate* with Salman. He would have to survive down here until Salman decided to invade, and then hope he didn't get caught up in the devastating crossfire.

He resolved to finish the job he came here for, despite the fact that it sounded like Kent might be leading him to a village of savages. If it was the same skull-faced savages he had encountered the other night, he would recommend they backtrack along the trail and try and intercept and ambush Joshua and this girl, Marai, as they made their way there.

Is the girl one of them?

Salman was right to be concerned about letting this boy live. Joshua was probably doing exactly what The Speaker feared most; uniting the people of this planet against Salman and preparing them for the invasion.

What about my present emergency: Why can't I move? I must have broken my connection to my brain stem, because I have no motor skills. Not even to speak.

"I don't know what to do!" Marai cried out. "Are you in a coma? Give me something, *anything!*"

I can still hear, so my audible nerves work, but I can't tell if my optical nerves work unless I can open my eyes again. I still can't move, and I still can't communicate with Marai. Is this where I give up on logic and reason and pray to a God I don't really believe in?

"I'm going to take your hand and you squeeze it if you can hear me." Marai said. Joshua heard her moving again, but he still couldn't feel anything. "Can you hear me?"

I can hear you, I just can't move or talk or feel! Joshua started to feel the panic set in again. He had a foreboding feeling that he would be like this forever, and he wished he could just be blinked out of existence, rather than suffer through a lifetime of blackness in this prison. *Help me, help me please!* Joshua wasn't sure if he was praying to a deity or pleading with Marai.

He heard Marai speak again: "I rebuke the Destroyer, for your sake!"

Suddenly, he could feel her hand in his. He

Salman wanted the denizens of this planet to be broken to the point that they offered absolutely no resistance when he came down. These "people," united against—and prepared for—their invaders would cause problems, and this boy sought to be their champion. Although, with Salman's superior technology, Sayid imagined wiping them out completely was the best option.

It's just as well. Nobody needs boogeymen running around.

"Are we going the whole way to the village tonight?" Kent asked.

"Yes," Sayid said. "Although why you won't take me to where Joshua is now is simply beyond me."

"I think we're going to need help," Kent said.

"Against a couple of teenage kids?!"

"Listen, I don't know if you had the distinct opportunity of dealing with this kid on The Exodus, but he's smarter than the average bear."

"Is he faster than a bullet?"

"The girl might be," Kent said.

"Get serious, Waller," Sayid said.

"I am, sir," Kent said. "Believe me, I think you'd be better off shooting first and asking questions later."

"What makes you think a village of savages would

nothing.

Obviously, my body is reacting to the alien bacteria in the water. My genetic code was created to ward off diseases found on Earth, but it has not evolved to understand how to process this new world, which has an evolutionary path completely different from my own. But what is it doing? Apparently, the synapses in my brain are misfiring. Right after Marai gave me the first drink of water, the shock of losing these connections must have threatened to shut my nervous system down entirely. With no connection to any of my life-sustaining processes, it's a miracle I was able to breathe long enough to live one day. Marai said I was like this for three days, so I must be reconnecting some of those neurons.

I can think now, but I couldn't hold a rational thought moments before. Do I still have access to my long-term memory? When's my father's birthday?

Joshua tried to recall his father's birthday, but couldn't remember.

Maybe it's because I didn't use Earth dates on the Exodus as much? Maybe it's just one of those things that I forgot because there hasn't been much use for it?

Then Joshua realized he couldn't remember his father's name, either.

That's worrisome. Okay, so my long-term memory is gone.

help us?"

"According to Marai, these savages hate them way more than they do us."

"And how do you plan to communicate with them?" Sayid asked.

"With loud words and wild gestures," Kent said. Sayid stopped walking and glared at him. "Sir," Kent added. This was not helping Sayid's bad mood.

"Marai's mom speaks English, so she can translate," Kent said.

"How could someone from this planet know English?" Sayid asked, skeptically.

"I really don't know, sir. Advanced intelligence?"

"Compared to you, that's everyone."

"Oh, you made a funny, sir! High five!"

Sayid punched him in the stomach and started walking again.

"Is someone following us?" Kent asked.

Sayid looked behind them as he walked. "I can't see anyone."

"You can't see that human-shaped shadow in the

Then suddenly, he was alert, awake, himself. As awake as he had been any other day of his life, with all his mental facilities intact. But the blackness was still there. Joshua tried to figure out why he couldn't move. Why his body wouldn't respond to any of his brain's commands. He started to be frightened as the time moved on and he wasn't able to do anything. He was a prisoner in his own body.

"Joshua, are you alive?" Marai asked. He could hear her and understand her, but his body might as well be someone else's, for all the control he had over it.

He tried shouting for Marai to help him, but the only sound he heard was in his thoughts. He could hear Marai moving next to him, but if she was touching him to check his pulse, he couldn't tell. Joshua was scared. More than he had ever been in his life. He started to wonder, too, if he was dead. He tried to shout again. He tried to visualize himself sitting up and telling Marai he was alive, but the scene just played out in an endless, frustrating loop in his head.

Get it together, Joshua! Try to figure out what's going on with your body. He forced himself to focus on the problem in a rational way, rather than panicking and accomplishing distance?" Kent asked. "The one that's making no effort to hide behind trees?"

Sayid looked back again. "I think you need some sleep."

"What have I been telling you this whole time?"

"Shhh!" Sayid said as he parted some leaves in front of him.

Before them was an ominous looking wooden wall adorned with skulls. Through a misty fog, Sayid could just make out a cliff wall looming behind it. Sayid crouched down and concealed himself behind a large plant. He looked over to tell Kent to hide, but Kent was not there. Sayid panicked and looked around desperately to find him.

He was nonchalantly strolling up to the gate. "Kent, get back here!" Sayid hissed.

"Hey, open up!" Kent yelled.

bunk. She looked under the bunk and pulled out a heavy jug filled with distilled water. The girl looked at her canteen and capped it, then pulled out a tin cup, rinsed it, and filled it with the water from the jug. She offered it to Joshua and he drank it, plopping his head down on the pillow and breathing heavily afterward. The water felt like cold, blue light running down his throat. He closed his eyes.

"You can oil dream water mother ship?" a voice asked. Joshua held onto the words vigorously until he understood their meaning. He knew this was important, but his brain kept wanting to slip down into darkness. *What was the voice asking? Why can't you understand, Joshua? Focus!!*

You can only drink water from your ship?

That was it! He had to let the voice know before he faded to black again! The blackness crept in around the edges of his vision until he swam in it. He tried talking, but he felt trapped inside his body. He couldn't move his mouth, or make any sound. There was just… blackness. He had no mastery over his body. He couldn't even tell if he was dreaming or awake, or if he could even understand the difference. He started to spin. *Wake up, Joshua!!*

15

The massive gate opened, creaking like an ancient coffin. Sayid shivered at the sudden chill that seemed to permeate the air. Through the mist, a pale-faced figure walked straight toward Kent. Sayid pulled his revolver from its holster.

That fool is going to get us both killed!

The skull-faced man stopped in front of Kent, and Kent stood there, apparently unperturbed by this ghastly figure. No words passed between them. The skull-faced man looked straight at Sayid—*were his eyes closed?*—and pointed to him. Sayid cocked his hammer back.

"He wants you to come, Sayid!" Kent yelled. "Don't worry, everything is fine!"

"He must be *crazy!*" Sayid whispered to himself.

"I think they know you're there!" Kent yelled.

Sayid felt someone standing behind him, and he looked back to see three skull-faced men standing behind

WOOD/LIFEBLOOD

"It's Marai," she said patiently, offering him the canteen.

Joshua grabbed the canteen, desperate to extinguish the fire in his throat. He started to weakly pour the water into his mouth, but then spat it out when he felt how thick it was. He wiped his mouth with his hand and then examined the liquid.

"This is blood!" he yelled. "You're trying to give me blood to drink!" He held up his hand in her face.

"That's because you're going to die with these people," the Council Speaker said.

"You!" Joshua said. "Their blood is on *your* hands!"

"Not my hands; yours," Speaker Salman said.

Joshua looked back down at his hands.

"It's only water," she said.

"It's only water," Joshua repeated.

Water. Somewhere in his mind, Joshua felt this was exactly right. What did that mean, though? "The water," he said. But what was he *saying?*

"Yes, drink some," the girl said. *Mary?* She offered the canteen once more.

"No," Joshua said. He pointed underneath the

him. None of them held weapons, but he could see up close that their eyelids were sewn shut, which caused him to shudder. One of them gestured for him to arise. He stood up slowly, still holding onto his gun. The same one gestured for him to walk to the village. He still had three bullets, which would clear a way for his escape, but then he remembered what happened to dead bodies around these men, and he decided to holster his gun and join Kent. The men walked behind him.

"See, I told you everything would be alright!" Kent said.

The gate swung shut behind them.

"They go inside a village," Tai said. "One of my people's village."

"How many of them were there?" Hugh asked, then added, "the Visitors," to clarify in case Tai saw some of the villagers also.

"I counted three," he said. "But one of them lag back for some reason."

"Did all three go in?" Hugh asked.

"Yes," Tai said. "Then they shut the gate. These

WOOD/LIFEBLOOD

"Who are you?" Joshua asked.

"I'm Marai," she said. "You've been sick like this for three days since the crash."

Sick? He had never been sick in his entire life. He was part of the Darwin Generation, created to be less-susceptible to sickness and aging! He couldn't *get* sick!

Someone turned off a switch, and the ship they were in suddenly started falling from the sky, and when it crashed into the trees, Joshua sat up, yelling.

"You're dreaming again," the girl—Marai?—said, pushing him back down onto the bunk. "You're delirious!"

"I'm sorry, I'm sorry, I'm suh…" Joshua said. His body was on fire, so he kicked the blankets off. "I need a drink."

The girl pulled a canteen out of her pack and opened it. Joshua couldn't think of her name, but he knew he was supposed to know it. He could see her name in bright colors, just out of reach, but every time he tried to catch it, it flew off.

"You're a connector," his dad said. "Your brain can see things nobody else can."

"Then why can't I remember her name?" Joshua asked. His dad turned into a girl.

guys are going to be in trouble!"

Hugh thought for a moment. "Is there a vantage point we can observe what's going on in there from?"

"A large cliff overlooks the village," Tai said. "We going to have to take the long way up, though."

"Lead the way," Hugh said.

This was probably the end.

Sayid would still fight to the death, because of the survivor in him, but he realized it would most likely end badly. He watched as villagers emerged from their huts to watch him and Kent. They stayed at a respectable distance, but the numbers of them continued to grow until they were completely encircled.

They came to a cliff face and stopped before an altar. If they expected him to just lie down on that thing…

A drum began to beat and a badly burned man emerged from the cave behind the altar. A swell of awful singing started, everyone on their own note. Kent seemed unfazed by all this, but at least he had stopped talking. He just stared forward with no expression. When the burned man drew close, Sayid started to make a desperate plan for

V

Joshua opened his eyes, realizing he couldn't remember falling asleep. He was sweating profusely, but was chilled to the bone. There was a loose blanket on the bunk next to him, which he grabbed and pulled back over him, shivering.

"Dad, can you get me another blanket?" he asked.

"Your dad's not here," a strange female voice said. "Joshua, you're really sick."

Joshua struggled to grasp onto the thread of reality that seemed just out of his reach. Random memories flashed through his mind, and some even seemed like real life, lasting for hours until he came to and realized they had just lasted seconds. Then the dreams came again.

"Rise and shine, son of mine," his father said. He opened his eyes again and saw a dark-skinned girl standing over him, dabbing his head.

escape in his head.

I kill their chief first.

The singing rose in pitch until it was almost a scream. Sayid prepared to spring into action. Then the chief raised his hands and the noise stopped.

"Shen-KYU-AR!" he yelled.

"Shen-KYU-AR!" everyone echoed. Then they all—including the chief—fell at Sayid's feet in a submissive position. Nobody made another sound or motion.

"What does that mean?" Sayid speculated aloud to Kent.

A woman's voice called out from a cage hanging above them all:

"It means, 'Executioner.'"

there's nothing. It's as if…" His voice trailed off and he got a distant look in his eyes.

Marai waved her hand in front of his face.

"Are you having a stroke?" she asked. Joshua snapped out of his stupor and looked at her with sadness in his eyes.

"They did it. They launched an EMP and took out the electronics. Probably worldwide."

"What's an EMP?" Marai asked.

"It stands for Electro-Magnetic Pulse. It's a weapon from Earth that can disable anything electronic. They must have launched it right before we fell."

"Who?" Marai asked.

"*Them.*"

16

The sun was just touching the top of the cliff when Hugh reached it. He had tied up his horses at the foot of the cliff near some water during the night, and continued the rest of the way on foot. He unslung his rifle and used the scope to look down on the village.

"They bad people, my family," Tai said.

"So you've said," Hugh replied, still looking around the village. Everyone appeared to be sleeping, still.

"Why don't you like them?" Borghaus asked. Hugh found it odd that Borghaus took *any* interest in Tai, so he set his rifle down and listened.

"They serve the Destroyer. They live they lives to kill and ruin."

"Didn't *you* set about on a killing spree?" Borghaus asked. "You didn't seem too opposed to killing *then!*"

"I was supposed to become a soul eater. They the men who like to sew they eyes shut to see spirits. With the feet with Marai's help, then tenderly made his way to the pilot's seat.

"I prefer my outside to be outside," he quipped, gesturing to the branch protruding through the windshield.

"Yeah, I imagine that would be hard to fly with," Marai came back. She watched as Joshua touched a few displays, then opened a panel underneath the yoke and turned a handle a few times. The handle made a high-pitched revving sound as it wound up. He pressed a button near the handle and nothing seemed to happen. Joshua looked concerned.

"Nothing," he said.

Joshua got up and opened a cabinet with tools in it, then used one of the tools to open a panel in the floor. He fiddled with some connections on what looked like a giant battery, and once again tried the handle under the yoke.

"We're not even getting a manual static charge," Joshua said.

"O-o-okay," Marai said. She had no idea what he was talking about.

"This handle I've been turning should create enough spark to at least light up the screens for a bit, but

Lamek, it is a great honor to become a soul eater. You dedicate you life to The Destroyer. No wife, no babies; no purpose except to kill.

"On the day I am to sew my eyes closed and take the blood oath, I get scared. I decide I would rather be a hunter or even *servant*. This didn't go so well with my tribe."

"Did they try to kill you?" Borghaus asked.

"No," Tai said. "That would be an honor. They throw me out. They tell me I can never come back to my family and friends.

"This hurt me bad, Borghaus. Real bad. I don't have nobody else. So I set off to prove my loyalty to the Destroyer. I do horrible things. I keep trying to kill bigger people to get back home, but nobody want me anymore. Nobody ever recognize me for trying to do what I am taught to do. I been a failure my whole life."

Tai hung his head.

"You're kind of ugly when you're sad," Borghaus said. "I like the pretty you better."

"I talked with the woman in the cage," Kent said.

Joshua looked down at his toes and wiggled them, then looked back at the screen. He tossed it aside.

"What's the matter?" she asked.

"It's not working. I'm not a doctor, but I've spent time studying medicine while on the voyage, and I think I might have a microfracture in my neck," Joshua said. "I feel a little tenderness in my neck, right on the spine. You were probably right to be concerned."

"What should we do?" Marai asked.

"Well, I'm not paralyzed, so that's a good sign. Tell you what, there's a neck brace in the next cabinet over. If I take it easy for a few weeks, I should be fine."

"A few weeks?" Marai started to panic when she thought of her mother coming back to a ravaged village. She knew they were probably stuck here until Joshua felt mobile enough to climb down the tree. Or maybe…

"Could you fix the ship?" Marai asked.

"I don't know," Joshua said. "I'm not sure why it failed in the first place. If you get me the neck brace, I'll take a look at it."

"Oh, sorry!" Marai said as she unlatched the cabinet and brought him the brace. She helped him put it on and cinch it up snugly. He sat up and slowly rose to his

"They're expecting Joshua and Marai tonight."

Sayid stirred in his bag. By the position of the sun, it must have been midday. *Did Kent even sleep last night?*

"How do they know?" Sayid asked. "As a matter-of-fact, how did *you* know to come here?"

"I told you, Joshua and Marai sent me out to locate her mom, expecting me to come back and tell them the next day. If I didn't come back, they said they would come after her themselves. The reason the Lamek know is because I told them. Well, they overheard me tell her."

"Waller, they don't speak English," Sayid said.

"Well, I don't know *how* they know," Kent said, "but they're sure making preparations as if they did. There are men sharpening knives, arrows, spears. The Speaker should be pleased to know we finished the job."

"*I* will finish the job," Sayid corrected. "*I'm* the Executioner, remember?"

"Are you going to forget that I got you an army? You promised me a settlement if I delivered him to you."

"Just like a mercenary," Sayid said. "Anything for a reward." Kent smiled.

Marai rolled her eyes at herself, then said, "Here, drink this!" She supported his head as he tried to raise his lips to the cup. He took a few swallows, then tried to sit up. Marai put a restraining hand on his chest.

"You might have a neck injury," she said. "You were hit in the head pretty hard."

He held still for a moment and then pointed to the lower cabinet to their left.

"Inside that cabinet is a tablet and a scanner. Can you get it for me?" Joshua asked. "Opening it is kind of tricky; you…" Marai opened the latch quickly, pretending she hadn't struggled with it just ten minutes prior. "Oh," Joshua said. "Yes, like that."

Marai wasn't sure what he meant by "tablet." There were all sorts of supplies in the cabinet. Joshua seemed to guess at her hesitation.

"The electronic tablet. It looks like a sheet of metal with a glass face." Marai located it and grabbed it. "The scanner has a handle and a wide face." She grabbed another item that looked like it might be the scanner. She brought the items over to Joshua and handed them to him. He tapped on the tablet's face and nothing seemed to happen. He tapped again.

"They look like they're making preparations for war," Hugh said. "Everyone seems to be readying weapons."

"This is no good, boss," Tai said. "You should leave before you get hurt."

"Something big is going to happen here; something history-making. I have to be here to witness it."

"And maybe judge some of my bad family?" Tai said.

"If it comes down to that, yes."

"I stay here with you, then, boss," Tai said.

"I didn't think you had a choice," Borghaus said.

"Yeah, but I want you to know I'm making the right one," Tai said.

"We'll see," Hugh said.

Sayid never felt so much power. He had always lived in the shadows of Salman, but now that *he* was the one people worshipped, it filled him with a strange sense of confidence. These people seemed attracted to strength and power, and Sayid knew he possessed both. Everywhere he walked in the village, people made still didn't respond.

Her makeshift ladder touched the ground beside her, and she tested its strength. It felt sturdy enough to climb. Before scaling the rope, Marai unhooked the tin cup from her belt she used for drinking and filled it with the crystal-clear water of the pool. She took a drink. It was a little warm, but it didn't taste bad. She filled the cup again and held it in her teeth as she grasped the knots of the vine rope and started to climb. Her arms burned when she neared the top, but having been in gymnastics her whole life, she was used to this kind of pain. She was wary pulling her upper body into the ship, and kept the rope wrapped around her foot, just in case. When she felt it was sturdy, she swung her free foot up onto the floor and pulled herself in.

Marai scooted over to Joshua's side and saw that his eyes were open.

"Are you awake?" she asked. He nodded.

"There's an emergency ladder next to the door." Joshua said in a weak voice. Sure enough, in slightly complicated, red English letters were the words "EMERGENCY LADDER," on a cubby opening next to the door.

offerings to him. They came out of huts or alcoves, holding out an offering to him in both hands with their heads bowed. Normally they were small arrowheads, knives, or animal skulls, things he didn't really have use for. One offering was really interesting to him, though; six spent hollow-point .45 slugs, splayed out and coated with dried blood. *His* slugs. They must have been retrieved from Grouch's dead body after they had left. *They admire my weapon. They have probably never seen anything so destructive!*

As he passed underneath a hanging cage, a woman said in English, "You can't kill my daughter." He stopped.

"Can't, or *shouldn't?*" Sayid asked. "Because I assure you, madam, I most certainly have the ability to."

"She's innocent! She has never intentionally hurt another person in her life," she said. "How can you justify killing an innocent child."

"It's not really her I want to kill," Sayid said. "It's the boy she's traveling with, Joshua, whom I'm interested in killing. If she stays out of my way, she has no need to die."

"She's not the type of person who would stand by and watch you murder someone in cold blood. She has already watched her own father go that way."

kicked off the bottom, desperate for air. It seemed like she would never reach the surface, when suddenly, she broke free and drank deep from the air above. She swam toward the shore gasping and aching. Her head pounded from the force of the water closing in on her when she had landed. When she reached the shore, she pulled herself up and just lay in the grass with her eyes closed against the sun streaming through the trees, breathing precious life back into her lungs.

When she felt rested enough, she opened her eyes and looked up at the ship lodged in the tree. It rested against an ancient trunk and was held aloft by two massive branches. She could see clearly that the settling-in that jettisoned her into the pool was all the movement the ship was going to make. It was wedged pretty solidly now. If Joshua could get it running again, they were going to have a hard time freeing it from the clutches of the tree. Who knew if it could even fly anymore? When she thought of Joshua trying to fix it, she realized he was still up in the ship.

"Joshua?" she shouted.

No answer.

She tried yelling to him again and again, but he

"I'm sorry to hear it, but *really*, can we get past the whole mourning for the loss of a loved one, already? In all of human history, haven't we learned that *everyone* dies? What does it matter when or how? Or at whose hands? It's going to happen, no matter what. I come from a whole planet of people to whom these arbitrary rules don't matter one bit! One day you're alive, the next you're dead, end of story. We only say we care about these things out of a sense of self-preservation, anyway. We say it's for the good of society, but ultimately, who benefits from such rules? *You*. It's *always* been for *you*."

"What a pessimistic view of life," she said.

"Do you have *any idea* how many people have tried to steal *my* life from *me?!* Justified or not, the end result would be the same if I hadn't done *everything* and *any*thing I could to outlive them! I'm alive today *only* because I realize the rules were written for other people! If your daughter dies, it will only be because she's too weak to break the rules," Sayid said.

"Those rules are what make us human! I'd rather my daughter dies upholding those rules than live like an animal," Kit said.

"As you wish," Sayid said.

WOOD/LIFEBLOOD

when it didn't. If the tree hadn't caught them, they might have both drowned in the water below.

She stuck her head out and recognized the tree as one the Tutek people used to make twine. The vines were very fibrous, and wove together very tightly. With no weaving, they were not that strong, though. She snapped off a few of the vines and started to braid a really long rope, tying knots every so often.

"I'm going to get you down from here," Marai said to Joshua. *Maybe he can hear me.*

She had to tie a few lengths together in order to make a rope long enough to reach the rainforest floor. She anchored one end to a seat, and tossed the other end out of the opening. While standing in the doorway, she turned and looked at Joshua, still lying unconscious.

How am I going to do…?

Before she could finish her thought, the ship settled slightly in the direction of the open hatch. It was just enough to cause her to lose her footing and she toppled out into the open air. She screamed until she hit the water with a loud slap below. The impact forced the remaining air from her lungs and she felt the water pressure increase until she hit the bottom of the pool. She

17

"Hey, boss," Tai said, "someone coming through the trees below."

There was barely enough light in the sky to make out some movement in the jungle near the village. Hugh looked through his scope and tracked the motion. Whoever it was seemed to be heading toward the village.

The Messengers, Jack said in his ear.

A lookout in a stilted hut inside the village made a noise like a bird. Hugh could see villagers moving about quietly a hundred feet below, then settling into dark places. Was this the war they were preparing for?

Someone near the wooden gate swung it open. Hugh looked through his scope at the two figures revealed there.

A boy and a girl?

Not just any boy or girl, Jack said.

They couldn't be any older than fifteen! What was

dabbed at the blood. "Joshua!" She checked his pulse and was relieved to feel his heart still beating in his neck. She quickly unbuckled him and struggled to lay him down on the ship's floor. She remembered hearing something about not moving someone if they had a potential neck injury, and immediately cursed herself.

"Joshua," she repeated. "I need you to wake up!" He still didn't respond.

Marai tried to think about what to do next. No answers came. *Why wasn't there any prophecy about what to do when I found The Chosen One and got in a shipwreck?*

Then it occurred to Marai, why would a branch be protruding from the window? Unless…

She tried pushing some buttons next to the door, but it didn't open. There was a red lever on the other side that looked like some sort of manual release. She pulled it and the door slid open. She stepped back immediately and tried to brace herself in case the ship started to fall again. There, in the dim morning light, she could see the pool the waterfall emptied into about 60 feet below. The branches of a large tree had caught them, but she didn't know how precariously they were perched. She tried rocking back and forth on her feet to see if it moved at all, and was relieved the uproar about?

They are dangerous, Jack said. *That's the same boy they refer to as the Wretched One, and she is the Seer. They are supposed to bring about the end, remember?*

The two figures walked into the village. The girl held onto the boy's arm, but she didn't look like she was *getting* support, but rather giving it. A figure stepped out from the cave directly below him and stopped in front of an altar.

"That's one of them I follow," Tai said.

"I've been watching him throughout the day," Hugh said. "He's worshipped by the villagers."

"I don't see the other two," Tai said.

"Shhh. I want to see if I can hear what they're saying," Hugh said.

Hugh strained his ears to hear the conversation that passed between them, but the slightest breeze made it impossible to hear anything. Just mumbling. The boy took a step forward, and the man threw something at his feet, which the boy let lay.

He's going to kill, Jack said.

"The boy is?"

"He speaks to Jack," Tai whispered to Borghaus.

IV

Marai woke up first, ears ringing. It took her a moment to realize where she was, and what had happened. Next to her, Joshua lay unconscious, blood dribbling from the one spot on his forehead unprotected by the helmet. A thick, twisted tree branch protruded from the windshield like a gnarled fist. Apparently, the windshield was strong enough to withstand reentry into an atmosphere, but not strong enough to withstand a direct blow from a sturdy branch. She felt gravity pulling on her from beneath, so she knew they had landed upright and it was safe to unbuckle herself. She immediately began looking for something to stanch the blood coming from her companion.

After a few frustrating moments of trying to discover how to unlatch the cabinets, she found some gauze and returned to Joshua.

"Joshua, can you hear me?" she said as she

Yes. He will bring about the deaths of many millions. He already has.

"Are you telling me this kid orchestrated the attacks on Hope?"

Yes. You must judge him now.

"He holds no weapon," Hugh said. "You know I can't judge anyone until they take up arms."

Use the rifle.

"I won't use the rifle. It doesn't matter *how* I kill, if I take a life preemptively it will cost me my ability to judge righteously."

It's for the good of the human race. This is what you were born to.

Hugh looked down at the boy. It was hard to believe he was such a threat. Then he noticed those in the shadows, along the wooden walkways, and in the cliff openings. They were all holding weapons aimed at the boy and girl. They looked far more threatening.

Still, there was the story from his father long ago. The cave paintings with the two people who were in the middle of the end of the world. If only he could remember any details! He had been so young when his father died...

"Go out and stand behind the man and the

contents. Maybe there was a clue inside as to where her daughter might be. Marai was clever enough to leave a message to her mom, should her mom come after her. Kit felt a glimmer of hope that her daughter was still alive and sending her a message! She approached the pack excitedly and grabbed the strap, pulling it off the branch. Suddenly, her feet were encircled by a coiled rope and she was violently flung into the air. She dropped the backpack in the process, and was immediately more concerned about that than she was about her own safety. When she came to rest, she found herself suspended upside-down from a large snare. Someone had set a trap for her or Marai, and in her haste, she had abandoned all caution.

She tried to loosen the rope around her ankles, but couldn't muster the energy to do so. She had exhausted all her energy running earlier. She felt the blood rushing to her head, making her eyeballs pound with pain.

Next to her, some brush popped. For a moment, she had the slightest hope that Marai had found her. That notion was quickly dispelled when she saw the skull-painted face of a man with his eyes sewn shut walking right toward her, wearing a gruesome grin on his face.

Then she blacked out.

children and prepare for my command," Hugh told Tai and Borghaus with urgency.

"Boss, you don't see?" Tai asked. There was fear in his eyes.

"See what?"

"They outnumber us. All they dead surround the boy and girl!"

"What?!"

"He's right, Hugh," Borghaus said. "We would never get through them all."

Even the dead know how dangerous they are, Jack said. *Now do what you were born to do!*

Hugh wrapped a hasty sling around his arm and started to lie down.

"If he draws his weapon on the boy, it will be too late," Hugh was startled to hear a voice off to his right. A man stood there, but he was tethered to someone unseen in the caves below.

"Who are you?!" Hugh asked.

"That doesn't matter right now! You have to shoot the man standing down there! Do it now!"

"He holds no weapon!" Hugh said.

He is not your concern!

She was not prepared to see Xrys' body disfigured as it was. His frail limbs were pinned to the ground with spikes, and his eyeballs were missing. His chest cavity appeared to have been opened and his heart removed, also. As shocking as it was, Kit still looked in the dark corners for any sign of her daughter. She took one last look at the poor man whose life had been so violently stolen, and walked out into the sunlight to resume looking for Marai.

The other warriors were kneeling beside loved ones, mourning loudly, as was their custom. She wanted to comfort them, but she still did not know the fate of her daughter. A thought occurred to her: *Where would I go to be safe if I were Marai?*

She looked up at the Sacred Mountain and ran to the trail at the base of the mountain. She knew Marai had spent a night in the cave near the top, and might go there if she thought she had nowhere else to go. About an hour later, Kit saw a glimpse of color on the trail up ahead. Her heart raced and she broke into a run again. As she got closer, she saw the color was from Marai's backpack, hanging from a branch on a tree.

Kit walked up to the backpack to look through its

"That's what I'm saying! I've seen him kill in the blink of an eye! You won't have time to react when he decides to move! It will be too late!"

End the boy's life now, Hugh!

Hugh was so conflicted. His lifelong, trusted companion was telling him to do something that was against his very nature; something Jack *knew* would result in the loss of Hugh's ability to judge forever. Now this stranger shows up and asks him to make the same sacrifice, only in defense of the boy and girl. Either way, he would have to take someone's life unjustly if what they were saying was true. Did he even have any reason to believe in either of them? He turned his attention back to the scene below.

Inexplicably, the girl vanished into thin air. Hugh looked around and noticed the villagers had all put down their arms for some reason, and were starting to stir. The man started walking a few steps to his right.

"He's going to draw any moment!" the man yelled. "Please save the boy!"

KILL THE WRETCHED BOY!!

Hugh had no answer, and his indecision froze him into inaction. Whatever went down, he would just be a *world is worth losing my Marai! How could I be so reckless? I've lost my husband already, and now my daughter! Please, God, not my Marai! Not my sweet Marai! I will give anything to have her safe! Take me, if you want, just let her be safe!*

The few miles to the village passed in a blur, and the adrenaline re-surged when Kit saw the smoldering huts and bodies strewn about, riddled with arrows. The warriors were all running to check on their families, and Kit ran straight to the hut where she had left her daughter. Marai was not in her bed, and some of her items were missing. Perhaps she had escaped?

She turned and started examining the bodies of those who had been killed. Her heart broke when she saw her friend, Xu, and Marai's friend Chetl lying dead near their huts. Near Atl's hut lie the bodies of many warriors, who had died protecting their chief. Apparently in vain, because Atl's body was nearby, with a hatchet still lodged in his back. The last place Kit thought to look was in the palsied Xrys' hut. He had become a mentor to Marai during the last month, and she was afraid Marai would have foolishly tried to save him in this attack. She paused for a moment at the entrance of the hut, and took a deep breath before pulling back the curtain and entering.

witness to, and then be forced to act *after* the damage had been irreparably, eternally done. He about gave up on doing anything until he felt a tug on his soul.

"We got this, boss," Tai said. "Loosen our tethers!"

Hugh watched in shock as Tai and Borghaus both leapt off the cliff and landed one hundred feet down into an invisible crowd. The mighty Borghaus swung his large fists, cutting a swath through the unseen enemy as Tai followed behind him, also battling unseen assailants. They were making their way to the boy.

Borghaus stumbled and fell, then lay flailing as his assailants pinned him to the ground. Tai still moved; ducking, spinning, and leaping. He was very near the boy.

When suddenly, he was stopped short. Falling to the ground with his hand outstretched, still a few feet away from the boy. Hugh felt their distance from him weakening their strength.

"You can make it, Tai!" Borghaus yelled.

With this encouragement, Tai mustered enough strength to fight to all fours and claw his way forward.

The man circling below cocked his elbow slightly.

"He's going to draw!" the stranger standing next

been smashed against the road, and was worthless to her now. She gathered a few of the remaining articles of clothing on the ground, stuffed everything into her backpack, and told the warriors she was ready to return to the village. No point in wasting any more time here.

After spending the night in a hasty camp, they all arose and began walking down the trail back toward the village. Partway through the day, the Tutek warriors started shouting and running up ahead of her.

One warrior ran back to her. "There is a fire, Kit!"

She immediately regretted leaving Marai, and the worst thoughts immediately filled her head. It didn't help when the trees broke before her by the lake and she saw the billowing smoke rising into the sky at the base of the Sacred Mountain, right where the Tutek village lay.

Adrenaline kicked in and Kit found herself racing alongside the warriors in a dead sprint. The village was yet a few miles away, but Kit had no intention of slowing her pace until she saw her daughter safe. A mournful sound filled the air, and Kit was only slightly aware that the sound was escaping her own mouth with each exhale.

Why did I bring her out here with me? No research in the

to Hugh shouted. "Don't let him touch his gun!"

Hugh, the Wretched One will bring death to us all! Shoot him where he stands!

Hugh had no idea what to do.

Tai yelled and gave one last effort to move forward. He shot his hand out and touched the boy's leg.

"I no enter in, boss!" he yelled. "He pure!"

Hugh made his decision in that instant. He passed judgment on the man, and the man crumpled into a heap, dead.

It was done.

Hugh knew he had passed judgment before the man had made the decision to act, before he held a weapon in his hand.

He felt his captives leaving, and all his tethers weakening. Some of them started to vanish from his sight, being unbound from their mortal connection. Hugh spoke aloud, "If any of you want to prove you truly deserve your freedom, help the children escape!"

They all leapt off the cliff and into the battle beyond the mortal veil. Hugh looked down and saw his connection with Tai fading. Tai still lay underneath an unseen mob, but he was looking straight at Hugh. He gave of her gear scattered about, as if everything had been rummaged through and then discarded when deemed of little worth. The interior of the cab had been burned, and only then did Kit feel remorse for the cab driver who had been killed while taking them to the remote village near Montsacre. Somewhere, in a village down the road, a family was wondering what happened to a father who worked daily to scrape a meager living from driving a car he probably saved up most of his life to afford. He would have been missing for about a month now, and the fact that the cab was still here indicated they probably didn't know where he was going the day he disappeared. This road was very rarely traveled, so his complete disappearance would be all-the-more confusing.

She also knew if she walked down the road a way, she might see his decaying corpse lying in the road with a Lamek arrow protruding from him. There was nothing she could do for him now. When she had left the cab, she had been more concerned with saving her daughter's life than getting him home. Now that she had time to think about it, it struck her as very tragic, indeed.

Most of her papers were long gone, but there were a few books lying about. Her recording equipment had

Hugh a thumbs up.

Hugh took off his badge and threw it down next to Tai, who smiled before he disappeared completely.

"You need to help me save the girl, sir!" The man still stood next to him.

"Who do they have you tethered to?" Hugh asked.

"Myself. I tried to help the kids, but the tribe captured me!"

Hugh realized this man must have been the third companion of the Visitors who lagged back—he had been forced from his own body and a usurper posed as him.

"Then you go down there and kick them right back out! Nobody has more right to your body than you. They only have as much power as you grant them."

"Will do, sir." He turned around and jumped off the cliff. After a second, Hugh saw his mortal body sprinting toward a priest, who had someone in his grip on the altar. There was a brief scuffle between the priest and the man, and Hugh could now see that it was the girl who was on the altar. She and the priest disappeared, then he reappeared, clutching his hand.

Hugh watched as the boy sprang into action, trying to free someone from a hanging cage. At this point,

III

Kit's march to the cab was pretty uneventful. She had expected to see some of the rival tribe's gruesome warriors along the way, but there was no sign of them. She shuddered as she remembered the Lamek soul hunter who, despite his eyes being sewn shut, had walked straight for her and her daughter as they huddled, frightened, underneath a waterfall.

She had confidence in the warriors the Tutek chief, Atl, had sent with her. He had assured her they were the best the village had to offer, so perhaps her traveling companions were enough to dissuade any attacks. Meanwhile, her daughter, Marai, was safe in the village, as Kit set out to return to their abandoned cab and recover the gear they had been forced to leave behind.

The trail connected with the road above where they were attacked, so they approached the cab from the front. When they were close enough, Kit could see much many of the villagers had recovered their weapons and began running toward the boy, who had succeeded in freeing the captive. Hugh lifted his rifle and aimed in on the villager nearest the boy.

So much for ever judging again, Hugh thought.

He took a breath, squeezed the trigger, and watched the villager drop off the far side of the walkway they stood on, clearing a path for the boy.

Suddenly, Hugh's vision started to blur. He felt like he was being pushed down into unconsciousness. He dropped the rifle, fell to all fours, and began to shake.

I think you just gave me the key to drive your body, Donovan's voice said from within him. *You are weak now, I can feel it! You just forfeited your life!*

Get out! Hugh screamed. But his mouth didn't move. He was being supplanted!

I think I'll enjoy being you! Donovan said. *You are taller than I was. Now I'm no longer a king without a kingdom!*

Hugh's right hand came up and patted himself on the cheek, condescendingly.

We'll see how you like being pushed down into the blackness, unable to control your own body! Moving where I move, looking at what I look at, eating what I eat! By the way, you eat like waterfall where she and her mother had hidden from the Lamek warriors a few weeks prior, frightened for their lives. It had seemed like a distant dream, but seeing that waterfall brought the memory back afresh.

"Here!" she shouted. Joshua winced with her yelling into the mouthpiece, and she apologized quietly. "Turn to the right, up this mountain, and we should come across a road with a broken-down cab on it."

He deftly maneuvered the ship to point to the right. He started forward, when suddenly the console flashed brightly and she heard a loud noise in her headset.

The dark trees underneath Marai's feet started rushing toward them as the ship fell out of the sky.

a pauper! There are far better things to eat than beans, you know. You will thank me later!

You have no claim…

Donovan cut him off. *I have* <u>*every*</u> *claim to property I conquer! I told you I was the stronger man.*

Your claim will be short-lived, Hugh said. *You'd be better off in a pig than in me in a few hours.*

What do you mean? Donovan asked.

Hugh answered Donovan's question with one of his own: *How do you feel right now?*

Hugh could feel the aging process beginning already, and knew Donovan felt it too.

What is going on? Donovan asked.

I'm dying, that's what.

But, you can't…

Oh, I not only can, I will.

Then I'll just judge another person and take <u>*their*</u> *remaining life,* Donovan said. *Just like you did with me.*

That's not how this works, Hugh said. *In order for you to be able to judge someone else, you need to be a just man…*

"…which you absolutely are not," Hugh spoke aloud when he felt Donovan's resolve weakening. "You are a murderer and a thief."

"Modified people?"

"Not anymore," he said. His gaze drew distant, and she knew this was a tender subject. "We can talk about all this later. Right now we need to find your mom." He put on a headset and had her do the same. Then, he started up the engine of the ship and pulled on the yoke. The rocking of the ship told her they were now airborne.

"Where do we go to find her?" Joshua's voice chimed in her ears.

"Follow this canyon behind us until we get to a waterfall. From there, we need to look for a mountain road off to the right."

Joshua turned the ship around and pressed a button on the screen. Bright lights filled the canyon in front of them as they started sailing over the trees of the jungle. Marai had been on commercial flights before, but this was exhilarating! The floor underneath her was clear, so it seemed like she was flying just feet above the trees. After a while, the thrill wore off and she started looking for familiar landmarks to guide them. Every so often she would catch a glimpse of the river through the trees, and knew they were on the right track.

Suddenly, the trees broke and she saw the tall

How are you pushing me out? Donovan asked, incredulous. *How can you be this strong?*

"Strength is not being able to enforce your will on another person, it's standing in defense of the weak. The only person you have ever tried to live for is yourself, and as such, you don't know how to share space with someone else. You're driving yourself out."

Hugh pushed himself to his feet and filled his lungs with air.

Enjoy it, Donovan, Hugh thought, *because it will be the last breath you draw.*

He blew Donovan out into the misty morning air.

Hugh looked down just as the boy, the man, and the freed captive escaped through the gate. He realized now how he had been completely wrong to assume the boy and girl were ever a threat to Hope. The fact that the tribal members who worshipped death and destruction wanted the boy and girl dead should have been his first clue. The kids weren't there to bring about the end of the world…

They were there to prevent it.

"Good luck," Hugh said as he watched them join the girl outside the gate and pass out of sight.

there are some good people, too, although I hate to admit they're in the minority. Some of the most ruthless people from Earth—the planet, not the god—are passengers on that ship. They left behind many others to die; those they believed were beneath them."

"What happened to the planet Earth?" Marai asked.

"A meteorite knocked it out of orbit toward our sun, and sent everyone on a ten-month scramble to find another home before they all burned up."

"So this is an invasion?"

"They didn't know the planet would be inhabited. They barely knew it was habitable. They had to set off toward this planet, hoping to perfect extended space travel *literally* on-the-fly. It didn't stop them from *preparing* to invade, though."

"There you are, referring to 'them' again," she said.

"I'm not originally *from* Earth," he said. "I was part of a generation genetically created on the ship to live longer, in case cryogenic freezing failed. All I've known my whole life is the inside of that ship, the Exodus."

"So there are others like you?" Marai asked.

18

Hugh crawled on all fours toward the lake's edge. He noticed his hands were frail and veiny.

He had managed to untie his horses earlier, when he could stand, then he removed the saddle, blanket, and halters, and slapped them hard on their hindquarters so they would run free.

He knew the end was near. He would die alone in the middle of nowhere. It was the most alone he had been in all his six-thousand years on planet Hope. He knew that when he died, the forgotten history of the planet died with him. Nobody else knew about the first city, and he wasn't sure anyone knew about the cave, either. He looked up at the mountain looming before him now.

Home.

He hadn't been back here since he was old enough to venture out on his own. The untimely death of his father had driven him from the city he had grown up in, down in the pilot's seat and strapped in. He beckoned for her to sit in the copilot's seat. She strapped in, not taking her eyes from him.

"You know how to fly this space ship?" Marai asked.

"I taught myself," he replied. "It's an observation pod, built to be like a mobile lab to study the planet. They have a whole fleet of them up on the… I'd guess you'd call it the 'Mothership.'"

"There's *another* ship up there?" she asked. "Where?"

"Right now it's on the dark side of your moon."

"What are they doing there?"

"I'm afraid they don't have good intentions," Joshua told her. "They believe you're a hostile species and plan on launching a preemptive strike to drastically reduce your population before they take over the planet."

"The way you're saying 'they' tells me you're not in agreement with this plan," Marai said. "At least I hope that's what I'm understanding."

"I'm sort of a fugitive right now," Joshua said. "There are some bad people up there who believe their survival can only persist with the destruction of others. But never to come back until now, thousands of years later. It was most likely in ruins now, as he heard it had been abandoned long ago. It looked like he wasn't going to make it back before life slipped from him. So much for laying his body down to rest near his father's final resting place.

Oh, well. He would see him soon enough.

He put his face into the lake and drank deeply. The water felt good going down his parched throat. When the ripples died down, he was surprised to see an old man with white hair looking back at him. He never thought he would see himself grow old. He glanced up from his own reflection and saw Jack standing behind him.

"You made a huge mistake," Jack said.

"Doesn't feel that way to me."

"Why didn't you listen to me?" Jack said.

"It felt wrong," Hugh answered.

"And what good has come of it, Hugh? Millions will die."

"Millions have already died."

"But the world hasn't ended. You enabled that to happen."

"It hasn't happened yet. I will let history judge the

II

Marai had never seen anything like the inside of Joshua's ship, being a regular teen from a regular school. She had her ideas of what an alien ship might look like from movies and her imagination, but this was a little less spectacular than what she envisioned. No consoles lit up with a million blinking buttons, no hovering, holographic images. Just a simple screen display and a yoke for the pilot. The rest of the ship looked like a camper, with bunks, storage cabinets and a small sink area. All streamlined designs, but not very "otherworldly," in her opinion.

Then again, the "alien" that came from the ship was a regular boy about her age, maybe 14 or 15. He didn't have green skin or an exoskeleton. No overly-large head and eyes. Definitely not slimy, and maybe even a little cute with his dark hair and piercing blue eyes.

She looked around for the pilot until Joshua sat

boy and girl."

"You don't even know their names," Jack said.

"No. But I realize who they are now." He pointed at the Sacred Mountain. "Six thousand years ago, a beloved Prophet drew the future of this planet on a cave wall. The Sign, the Seer, the Connector, and the two sides at war. I remember now. Encircled about by… a village wall, I guess. I can't believe I lived long enough to see it come to pass. Honestly, I was starting to think it would *never* come." Hugh lay down in the grass and rested his eyes.

This isn't the end, Jack said. *Not even close.*

"Glad I won't have to endure any of it physically," Hugh said.

He looked up and saw a sliver of the moon in the blue sky.

"I know who you are," Hugh said. Jack didn't answer.

"Don't have a mortal body or a spirit one, that I can see; except for when I look at you indirectly. You exist everywhere, like a force of nature. A *Destructive* one."

Congratulations. You've found me out. Thanks for doing my killing for me all these millennia.

"Oh, I wasn't doing it for you. I was doing it for

"I don't know if we're *supposed* to do anything," Joshua said. "I didn't intend to meet anyone down here; as a matter-of-fact, I was hoping to avoid *all* contact with any intelligent life. But like I said, now that you're here, I might need your help figuring out how to survive here."

"Oh," Marai said. Joshua noticed her posture sag just a little. "Well then, if you are just as confused as I am, maybe I can get you to help me do something important."

"Sure," Joshua said. "Anything you need."

"I need you to help me find my mom."

the people of this planet."

Whatever you believe, the end result is the same; death.

"Except I prevented more death by taking the lives of killers. I allowed far more people to live. Which begs the question: Did you teach me how to judge only so you could manipulate me into using my powers just to hasten whatever is coming? For this one moment depicted on the cave wall concerning those two kids?"

That "moment" hasn't yet come to pass. I was just trying to get ahead of it.

Hugh's breathing was becoming labored.

"Oh, so you know how it's going to end? You're actually increasing your efforts to stop it, so I'm guessing it doesn't end well for you."

So far, your precious "Prophet" has been right, but I have a plan to disrupt your perfect balance. All the pieces are in place…

"You will lose," Hugh said.

Ask the people left behind on Earth if I lost.

"Huh," Hugh said. His breath was now intermittent wheezes.

"Well, then, I just have one more thing to say to you."

What's that?

Joshua couldn't believe he hadn't introduced himself yet. He had been so caught up in trying to figure out what was going on, he'd forgotten his manners completely.

"I'm Joshua Hawker," he said.

"My name is Marai Gardner," she replied. "I think we were destined to meet."

Joshua recalled how the landscape had guided him to land his pod in this spot, and couldn't think of a rational reason why or how. He had a hard time with "destiny." He believed his own actions were all that accounted for how his life played out. He could have just as easily chosen to ignore the earthen signs and thus rewritten his "destiny" as he saw fit. Or perhaps his brain was just desperate to make a connection so he interpreted things that were not there. Or it could all just be a series of coincidences? Very, very *convenient* coincidences? But how would that explain this girl being here at this time?

"Perhaps," Joshua replied. "Regardless, it's nice to meet a native of the planet who can help give me some answers."

"You don't know what we're supposed to do?" Marai asked.

"I rebuke you in the name of the Creator."

. . .

Hugh felt a stillness in his heart that he hadn't ever felt before.

He closed his eyes once again, and only opened them when he heard footsteps approaching in the grass. He saw a tall figure with long, pure white hair standing above him. The figure was dressed in only a loin cloth. Hugh could make out the shape of an hourglass around his eyes.

He bent down and touched Hugh lightly on the forehead.

Who are you?" Hugh asked. "You look… familiar." He could feel his body getting lighter, as if he were starting to float off the ground.

"I am the Gardener," he said, softly.

"I will take your vessel to its resting place," he said. "You may let go now. You have served Creation well."

He felt a deep peace. Hugh stopped seeing with his mortal eyes, and he began to discern a path stretched out before him. He wondered where it led, and took his first step down the path.

Not from the ship. So she was a native of this planet, but speaking English. This caused even more questions to arise in Joshua's brain.

"How did you get here?" he asked.

"My mother and I flew, then rode in a cab, and then walked—or ran, really—It's a long story."

"No, I mean, how did you get to this planet?"

"I've lived here my whole life," she said.

Joshua recalled seeing the lights of civilization on the planet's surface from the monitors of the ship, and now he knew the intelligent beings on the planet were human, or humanoid. He realized they must have been there for hundreds, if not thousands, of years. It made no sense. They couldn't have come from Earth because Joshua's ship was the first and only interstellar voyager to escape before Earth was destroyed from being knocked out of orbit by a meteorite.

But speaking English... it seemed too much of a coincidence that two languages could evolve on different planets to be so similar. Maybe her people could interpret and translate languages with their advanced intellect, or they had some technology that allowed…

"Do you have a name?" she asked.

Ahead of him, Hugh could now see the glowing outlines of familiar people walking toward him.

Hugh died, not alone.

THE END

I

"Are you the one I'm supposed to meet?" the girl asked.

Her accent was strange, unlike any accent Joshua had heard in his life. The musicality of it was different, with rises, falls, cadences, and pauses in unexpected places. The way she said "supposed to" sounded more like a single word, "spozeta," but Joshua could understand it, nonetheless. One thing was for sure: She was definitely speaking English. His brain raced to understand how someone from a different planet could be speaking in his native tongue.

"Are you from the ship?" he asked.

"What ship?" she responded. "*You* came from a ship."

"So… you're not from Earth?"

"Earth, like the constellation named after the ancient god?" She looked really puzzled.

Acknowledgements

I really debated whether I should put an acknowledgements section in these books, because I don't want to make people think they've read this in the wrong order. There is no right or wrong way, but the way *you've* read it is definitely right! Anyway, I just decided to put two different acknowledgements sections on both sides, that way, they match! (Just like I had to put two barcodes on the book cover so nobody thought one side was the "back.")

Also, this might prevent those snoopy people from cheating and reading the other ending first, amirite?

These books have been a doozy to write! I have so many notes and diagrams, helping me get the events in the correct orders and filling in gaps that each story might have that the other can provide answers to. The first book, in particular, was an exercise in restraint, even though I wanted to tell the reader *everythingrightnow!*

Unfortunately, the reader had to learn at the pace the characters did. It would make no sense for the author to pop his ugly head in and start 'splainin' stuff. But I hope the ending was a surprise that got your wheels a-turnin'!

IMPORTANT AUTHOR'S NOTE

This book is comprised of two separate but connected stories. You may start with either story and then flip the book over and read the other. Depending on which side you start on, the title is either *Blood Life*, or *Lifeblood*. Your experience with the stories might differ from someone who has read it in the opposite order.

So make your choice…

My whole goal in writing these was not to produce a gimmick, but to tell a story in a unique way from two different perspectives. If the end result is that readers are interacting with their books a little more, so much the better! There's always other ways of looking at things, and sometimes we fall into the trap of thinking "different" is "wrong." There's always two sides to a story, so let's talk about it!

That being said, it might help if you read the stories more than once. If you have a fresh perspective on how the story goes, you can go back and fill in the gaps. This story especially has many things that are only explained from one point-of-view, and if you find that section in the other side, you could get the complete picture. It works better here, because the stories take place in the same basic timeline and setting.

I recently got a professional review of my first book, wherein the reviewer said, "I alternated chapters, which works, too." This surprised me, but apparently, it works! I guess you could do it like that, but I'd personally be amazed at your capacity to follow multiple storylines. Maybe I'll go back someday and re-read everything that way.

DEDICATION

To Doug Wood
My bestest buddy growing up.

Now for some actual acknowledgements:

These books would not be possible if it weren't for a benevolent God in Heaven who knows my name and has inspired me in so many ways. The talents I was born with are gifts from Him; all I've done is work to develop them.

I would also like to thank my patient, loving, beautiful wife, Brenda, for standing by me, even when I might be undeserving of her. She's truly my muse; the person I run all my thoughts by first… and her advice is always excellent! Without her, I'm half a person.

I would also like to thank my kids for encouraging their ol' man to keep writing! They also read my books and give me valuable feedback, even catching the occasional typo! (I can still beat them in basketball, though.)

I would like to thank my neighbors and friends for being my smart readers, too! (And it delights me to hear them debating theories about my books with one another. Yay, the books work!)

Hey, I just had an idea: Let's throw in a fake ending to throw off the cheater who skips to the last page first!

"But whom, exactly, do we arrest?"

"Simple," he mused, musingly. "The butler did it."

"But the butler *always* does it!"

"Fine!" he raged, fuming a seething hot volcanic spew of aggression, his face as rouge as the cherry's. "Then it was the maid!"

"That's better," she approved, approvingly.

A monster bit their heads off.

THE END

Lifeblood

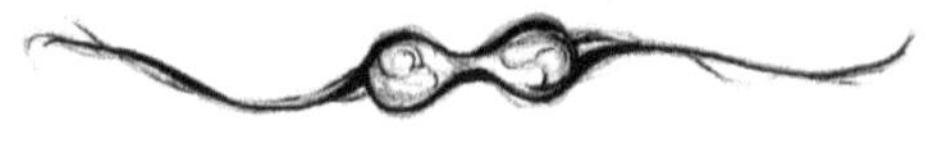

Turnabout Volume II

RUSS WOOD